Shadow Play

Jeffrey B. Burton

Pocol Press
Clifton, VA

POCOL PRESS

Published in the United States of America
by Pocol Press
6023 Pocol Drive
Clifton, VA 20124
www.pocolpress.com

Publisher's Cataloguing-in-Publication

Burton, Jeffrey B.

  Shadow play / Jeffrey B. Burton. – 1st ed. – Clifton, VA : Pocol
  Press, 2005.

    p. ; cm

    Short stories.
    ISBN: 1-929763-19-0

    1. Horror fiction. 2. Short stories. I. Title.

PS3602.U786 S53 2005
813.6–dc22   0502

These stories are fiction. Any inference to any person, living or dead, is
purely coincidental.

Dedication

This collection of short stories is dedicated to my daughter, Maddie Rose. When Maddie was a little girl she confessed to being terrified of her shadow…and so I gave her a reason to be.

Advance Praise

A lot of short fiction comes across my desk. When a Jeffrey B. Burton submission enters my Inbox, my pulse quickens. I know a Burton tale will take me down un-expected alleys. No one sees the world quite the way he does. Late at night, when I can't sleep, I feel that his vision might just be close to reality. Still, I keep coming back for more. Burton is the master of the twist ending...no, make it the master of the twisted twist ending.

Burton breaks the mold. The reader is often unsure which character wears the white hat and which wears the black. Like in real life, his characters wear many hats. When his characters put on the black hat, watch out, nasty things happen: the loving dad with the late night *hobby*. The *annoyed* downstairs neighbor, the *good* cop, the academic, all these people and more, inhabit Burton's rogue's gallery. Evil often has an ordinary face, perhaps even the face that tucks you in at night. Other times, evil really is the monster in your closet.

Burton has a way with children. He knows how the love for a parent can inspire his child to try his darndest to make the world right. He also knows how dangerous power can be in the hands of someone too young for a fully developed moral sense. There is a reason the most brutal armies use children as troops. Burton understands.

I recommend the *Shadow Play* collection. Let's keep Burton typing...and away from heavy blunt objects, sharp knives, and weapons of mass destruction.

-Raymond Coulombe, Editor, Quantum Muse

Shadow Play is as entertaining as it is chilling. Each tale is a journey through a dark and twisting maze, where illusion and reality are often one and the same. A work horror fans can really sink their teeth into!

-Dennis Kirk, Editor, Outer Darkness

The book you hold in hand is filled with twenty truly original and shadowy tales on the cutting edge of modern horror and suspense. These stories capture the dark reality we all fear, at once eerie and haunting, chilling and nightmarish.

– D. E. Davidson, Editor, Night Terrors Publications

Stories Previously Published

Shadow Play was published as *The Convergence* in the Autumn 1999 issue of *Outer Darkness Magazine.*

Shadow Play was published as *Silhouette* in the May 1998 issue of *Millennium Science Fiction & Fantasy.*

Eykiltimac Stump Acres was published in the Summer 2000 issue of *Potpourri Magazine.*

Per Diem was published in the Summer 1998 issue of *The Cozy Detective Mystery Magazine.*

Per Diem was published in the December 2003 issue of *Detective Mystery Stories.*

Free Toy Inside was published in the November 2002 issue of *Quantum Muse.*

The Tenth One was published in the December 1997 issue of *Millennium Science Fiction & Fantasy.*

Entitlement Cuts was published in the Fall 1998 issue of *Satire Magazine.*

The Inheritance was published in the Winter 1999 issue of *Crimson Magazine.*

The Inheritance was published in the December/January 1997 issue of *Millennium Science Fiction & Fantasy.*

The Bump-Bump Man was published in the March 1997 issue of *Millennium Science Fiction & Fantasy.*

Clippings was published in the Spring 1998 issue of *The Cozy Detective Mystery Magazine.*

The Forever Stone was published in the July 2004 issue of *Quantum Muse.*

Table of Contents

Shadow Play

The guards were pouring into the cell just as Webber's scream abruptly ceased. I knew they were expecting to break up yet another one of Webber's fights. The prison guards were startled to discover me lying motionless on the top bunk watching Webber, eyes bulging, kicking his feet frantically, blankets corkscrewed about the foot of his bed, doing a bizarre, ever-slowing, horizontal dance atop his bed, pulling ineffectually at his throat, as though choking silently upon a chicken bone.

Oh, but I'm getting ahead of myself...

Once there was a little boy. An only child. Friendless. Neglected by his parents, he would entertain himself for hours in his closet. With the help of a table lamp, minus its shade, the little boy would make endless shapes on any of the three narrow walls. Sitting cross-legged, alone, he'd pattern and mold his agile little fingers into the shapes of hawks, tarantulas, horses, sharks, spaceships, you name it and the little boy could craft it, flexing his fingers to near impossible angles in order to view new images on the whiteness of his closet wall.

The last time the little boy created these shapes in his private theater, he was ironing out the arched eyebrows of a Forest Owl with the curves between his thumb and forefinger when he noticed something odd about the wall. The shadow of the owl ceased to be flat. The shadow appeared to be made up of tiny, textured ripples, strangely three dimensional. The little boy blinked his eyes repeatedly. It didn't help. In fact the shape appeared to be moving, almost imperceptibly, as though breathing.

Shocked, the little boy dropped one arm to the floor. The wall shadow immediately turned into the figure of the small boy's remaining hand. Well, almost the figure. *It can't be,* a voice inside told him, *it simply cannot be.* The thumb on the wall shadow was on the opposite side from the one the little boy held in front of the light bulb. The little boy was frightened but glued to the spot. Eyes wide, he was transfixed by this new image. He slowly extended his palm. The wall shadow seemed to bubble outward in order to meet his touch. He wanted to scream, to run away, but couldn't.

The shadow, an inch off the wall, beckoned. They touched. The shadow was cold, almost metallic. It circled his hand in a tight grip. He felt its curiosity, its strength, its something elseness not quite as pleasant. The little boy pulled back. He knocked over the lamp with his flailing free hand.

1

The bulb smashed on impact, sending shards across the hard wood floor. The shadow grip disappeared and the little boy ran from the closet to the security of daylight, of the known world.

The little boy told no one. Who would have listened to him anyway? In time he came to believe it was a dream...

I was that little boy.

Most of Junior High was spent trying to blend into the woodwork. I did my fashion best to wear things that wouldn't call attention to myself. I'd sit strategically toward the teacher in order to be safe from the guys in the back row, but not too close as to be targeted as the teacher's pet. In gym class, although picked last for team sports, I worked hard so as not to call attention to my complete lack of sports prowess.

But it was bound to happen. Whenever a cow strays from the herd, he becomes easy prey for the coyotes and wolves. And the stragglers on the fringe, in my school, would eventually come face to face with one particularly mean coyote named Dick McCarthy.

McCarthy wasn't so much big as he was intense in his sadism. One year older, he was the bane of all seventh and eighth graders. His gang of bully-creeps would egg him on into messing with someone for no apparent reason. I once saw him haul off and punch a kid in the back of the head only because the poor sap was carrying his trombone to band class. McCarthy's assaults, if ever caught, would only merit him a day's suspension, which he seemed to relish. Even teachers were afraid of Dick McCarthy. Welcome to our public schools.

I'd made it through most of seventh grade without McCarthy taking notice of me. But on the day I straggled from the herd, I never saw it coming. Lunch had just ended and I headed to the restroom. After my business, I washed my hands, turned to leave and...there stood Dick McCarthy, surrounded by three of his bully-creeps.

"Okay now Piss Face," Dick grinned ear to ear, pointed a tube of something at the floor by me and squirted a gob of transparent liquid near my feet, "here's the deal. You're either gonna step in that gunk or I'll Super Glue your lips to the shitter."

That met with a chorus of glee from the bully-creeps. This must be virgin territory for Dick. He'd probably just lifted the Super Glue from the art supplies. At a complete loss for how to deal with this situation, I grinned back. I thought I might be able to ingratiate myself to the sociopath by pretending it was all so very funny. By pretending I was of his ilk. By being in on the joke. It didn't sell.

2

"Don't give me teeth, you little faggot. I'll punch your goddamn head off."

Dick's smile had disappeared. He reached over and pushed the tube hard against the top of my shirt, starting at my shoulder blade and laying a tight, scratchy bead diagonally down across my bony chest and stomach, ending above my belt. McCarthy had pressed so hard against me that I could feel the moisture of the glue begin to stick to my skin. It was not going to be pretty when the time came to take this shirt off. But I had a far more urgent issue to attend to. McCarthy emptied the rest of the gunk over my shoes. Snags of adhesive landed on them as well as the floor about me. He flicked the crushed and empty tube, cigarette-like, into the nearest urinal.

"Step in it right now, Piss Face, or I'll make you lick it up."

My heart was beating so fast, I felt it catch in my throat. There was no way I could cut and run. The bully-creeps blocked the only exit door. Just live through it, I thought. He'll be on to someone else tomorrow. The Super Glue won't hurt your shoes. But if you do anything other than exactly what Dick says, you're going to be eating his fist. Just live through it. It's just another toll you get to pay along the road. I stepped onto the fresh Super Glue and felt the glob squish beneath the sole of my right tennis shoe.

Dick cocked his head in the direction of the bully-creeps, "I told you momma-puss-boy would do it."

They all laughed. Dick was chuckling out loud now. Another one taken care of. Another kid tossed onto the heap. People like Dick McCarthy steal all your dignity. I was a puny ninety pounds soaking wet. My hair didn't part right, I wore thick glasses, and all I wanted to do was make it through the day. Just make it through another day without anyone noticing. No tall order there. But the Dick McCarthys of the world won't allow you that. They'll scar you. They'll burn it deep into your soul, until, on your death bed, instead of thinking about loved ones and better times, you'll find yourself gasping your last breath while fixating on how the Dick McCarthys superglued your K-Mart dress shirt to your hairless chest, then superglued your foot to the shithouse floor. And all the while it happened you didn't say boo and you didn't say peep.

At that moment in time I did a very impulsive, very stupid thing. I leaned forward and gave Dick McCarthy a shove. Off guard, and off balance, Dick fell backwards, landing on his rear end. All bully-creep laughter came to an abrupt halt. Dick glared up at me, eyes burning with hate. I accepted the inevitable. I was going to, most likely, land up in a hospital. I didn't know how to fight, much less how to hold my fists. I wasn't even going to try. Perhaps then the beating would go quicker.

"You're dead now, Piss Face, you're dead." And with my immediate fortune told in a non-too-subtle manner, Dick McCarthy started to rise.

Here it gets a little bit like the retelling of a car accident, where you can remember everything in perfect slow motion. Dick's mouth suddenly popped open in a perfect O, like that famous Edvard Munch painting, and he sank slowly back to the ground. The bathroom echoed with his extended, piercing exhale. McCarthy began to writhe in pain, on the dirty tile floor, as though having an epileptic seizure of some kind. We all stood over him in shock, as though waiting for some kind of warped punchline.

"Get help," yelled what must have been the lieutenant bully-creep as the other two jettisoned out the door, seeking out an authority figure for the first time in their lives.

Dick's eyes rolled back in his head, exposing the whites. The lieutenant bully-creep bent to help as Dick began to regurgitate his recently eaten lunch over his black T-shirt. I looked away, down at the floor. Something was happening here, but what? That's when it caught my eye.

The shadow, emanating from my feet, was moving on its own. I watched frozen with fear, and fascination. The shadow curved at a grotesque angle. A boomerang of darkness moving sideways, impossibly toward the light as it stretched forward to snare Dick's leg. The tendon-like shadow image, that now gripped Dick's ankle with an unforgiving power, tethered outward from me. It was my natural silhouette up to my thighs, then played tricks with its dark reflection as it taffied across the bathroom tile and connected with Dick McCarthy's lower leg. I saw the dark shade as it wrapped itself tighter and tighter about McCarthy's ankle. A deadly Boyscout knot that forever closed. Dick's blue jeans, skin and bone were being squeezed inward like a child clawing at putty. The memory from my childhood returned, and with it the assurance that it had certainly not been a dream. I stood there, riveted to the floor, right up to the stomach turning crunch before I tore my tennis shoe up from the floor and fled the rest room.

Dick McCarthy was gone for a month. When Dick returned he wore a cast up to his kneecap for the rest of the school year. He limped along with the aide of crutches. You could almost hear the seventh and eighth grade breathe a collective sigh of relief. Dick looked as though he'd lost thirty pounds, his face gaunt, white, much older. The story was that he had fractured his ankle by twisting and falling down on it.

But he and I knew differently. We both knew that something else, something definitely not an accident, had occurred that afternoon in the school restroom. I thought McCarthy might come looking for me, but neither he, nor any of his bully-creeps, ever crossed my path again.

4

There have been a handful of other occurrences throughout the years. Mostly in times of danger. I remember a sailing course from ten years back. Thought it might be a good way to meet people, to force a hobby. When the instructor took us out that first day, I felt a wave of nausea wash over me. Lightheadedness. I stared into the water, at the lapping, frothing greenness and hoped not to lose breakfast. The boat hit a hard wave and I toppled, headfirst, into the lake.

Only I never hit the water. An arm, quick and strong, wrapped about my middle and pulled me back on deck. I turned around to thank whoever had miraculously saved me from a cold, mid-afternoon dunking. No one was there. No one even remotely by me. Just a twisting shadow at my feet, blending back into what would be my logical reflection. The instructor, across the stern, blinked his eyes as though he'd just seen a ghost. I never returned for further courses.

Most recently was last Spring when Mike Cusack, the new Department Manager, had me stay late in order to reconcile the month-end HoustOil spreadsheet, a project for which I was not responsible. Just a little clean-up on the HoustOil account, Cusack had explained earlier that morning, just a little clean-up. Cusack's little clean-up found me still there late into the night. It made me miss Jonathan Pritchard, the firm's founding father, all that much more. The business had taken some drastic turns for the worse ever since Jon lost his bout with cancer.

I called Brook periodically, in order to tell her I'd be home late, but kept getting the answering machine. Another girl's night out, I figured. I walked the desolate skyways till I came to the elevator above the parking garage. Footsteps fell in line behind me. I heard the talk, the intimidating gang jive, obviously turned up a notch or two for my benefit. Street punks. I didn't dare look. I've spent a lifetime of avoiding eye-contact, an innocent look could prompt certain undesirable actions. I pressed the down button repeatedly until the elevator doors slid open. They followed me inside.

I stood with my back against the wall, head down, and listened to their obnoxious banter. Best to completely ignore them; appear absorbed in one's own thoughts, until something concrete occurs. Then, after the appropriate protocol has been established, hand over wallet and car keys. Whether they were trying to have some fun with me or were simply getting up the moxie for a real shakedown, the one with the serpent tattoos plastered over his thick forearms cracked wise about hitting the stop button "so then we could all become well acquainted."

I stared down at my feet. The light in the overhead bulb should have plastered any shadows against the wall at my back. But the ropes of darkness falling below my trenchcoat and starting at my feet weaved impossibly

5

forward, wrapping and slithering lightly about their legs, like tentacles about prey. These shadows emanating off of me bore no resemblance toward any earthy posture I could imagine. And I knew, with utmost certainty, that if these unwashed punks stopped the elevator or if they had pushed their intimidation game one inch further, that they would receive the biggest and, perhaps, last surprise of their lives as we all became very well acquainted, indeed.

After a breathless eternity, the elevator doors opened and they stepped off onto their level.

Mike Cusack's unexpected e-mail informed me that I needed to cut the Atlanta trip short in order to meet with him at nine sharp the next morning. There were some important changes coming down the pike that he needed to communicate. Something was up. With the loss of the CompCo account, the rumor mill had been steadily grinding for weeks. I switched to a much earlier flight, got back home in the afternoon...and there was stubble in the bathroom sink. Brook's bathroom. The one connected to the master bedroom. The one I never use. All my shaving supplies are kept in the downstairs bathroom.

Brook and I have been married almost two years. I met her at the diner where she waitressed. She was twenty, I in my early thirties. I fell in love with her. Or, perhaps, I fell in love with the absence of loneliness. What's the difference? I'd offered her a chance to leave a job she hated, to drive a better car, to make a home with all the trimmings. I knew that tilted love in my favor. Maybe I'm greedy, but I wanted people to see that this quiet, gawky outsider might possibly be human after all, and, for the first time, the very first time, think that he might just fit in.

This last year Brook has been out with her girlfriends several nights a week. 'Girl's night out' she calls them, and they'd become more frequent. I went out on a couple of these at first, but felt silly, felt my age. I didn't want to smother her. I thought she could get the night life out of her system. Brook would come home around midnight. Smelling of rum and coke, she'd slip into bed next to me and fall quickly asleep. Brook always thought I was sleeping. But I never was. Not once.

Barely comfortable with myself, it's much harder with others. I don't know how to behave in a relationship. I've not had any experience before Brook. I know how it must appear from the outside looking in, but from inside, I'd found a certain contentment. And now, home early from a business trip, I discover stubble in her vanity sink.

"Hey, Grandpa," Brook looped around the corner. "You're home early."

Sometime lately Brook had taken to calling me 'Grandpa.' She'd say it in a jocular, teasing manner. I pretended not to take it in the manner in which she most likely meant. Just another way of avoiding eye contact, I guess.

"How was the trip?" Brook asked.

"I'm tired." I stared at her. I could sense her anxiety.

"Why don't you lie down for a bit."

It was then I noticed something on the wall behind her, saw the darkness begin to blend, to move silently as it curved downward and swirled about her legs, a hush of black slithering up her jeans, across her stomach, her breast, angling toward her pretty, exposed neck.

"God no!" I squeezed between her and the bathroom door, took the steps two at a time. "Oh God, no!"

"What the hell has gotten into you?" Brook followed after me.

"Stay there!" I hurried toward the garage. "I left my briefcase in the car. I need to finish the actuaries."

"Jeeze, Grandpa. You almost ran me over."

Hours later, when I came back upstairs, the sink had been rinsed sparkling clean. You could even smell the cleanser.

"You're firing me?" I shook my head in disbelief.

"Roark," Mike Cusack sailed onward, a Cusack decision had been rendered, now it needed to be implemented, then off to the club for a round of golf, tell his rich pals how he'd made the executive decision to fire the company nerd. "It's called downsizing. With the loss of CompCo, we've been forced to re-evaluate our staffing needs in a manner best suited for our existing client base."

"But I've got seniority. And Mr. Pritchard always gave me excellent evaluations." Jonathan Pritchard, he of the Father-Christmas eyes, he who had founded this firm in the late fifties, and had built it into what his idiot son, with the help of his idiot son's fraternity pal, Mike Cusack, were rapidly pissing away. CompCo had quickly pulled anchor after outside auditors had given their account a less than flattering evaluation. Lucky we didn't get fined.

"There were a lot of factors involved in this decision, Roark." Cusack scooped together all the superficiality that was his essence and looked me in the eye, "Quite frankly it was the hardest decision I've ever had to make because of the tremendous staff we've got onboard."

"I never touched the CompCo account. If I'd still been doing the cross-reviews, like Mr. Pritchard had me doing—"

"Times change, Roark. Old man Pritchard's been dead over a year now."

7

Old man Pritchard? Where did this jargon-filled, let's-do-lunch SOB get off referring to Jonathan Pritchard as "Old man Pritchard?" "Old man Pritchard" had built this company up from scratch while you were busy filling your diaper full of your mission statement. "Old man Pritchard" had set up controls and safeguards in order to stop the lazy slop that passes for what happened with the CompCo account. "Old man Pritchard" had also, a dozen years ago, taken a chance with a young Icabod Crane look-a-like who'd bumbled his way through the job interview with nothing but a pocket calculator bouncing about in his otherwise empty briefcase.

"My work has been spotless. This is a business and the work product has got to count for something."

"Roark," Cusack patronized and peeked at his gold Rolex, "don't beat yourself up."

"If my work is excellent, and I've got seniority...Then what is it?"

"Roark—"

"No," I mustered my remaining courage. "What is it? I need to know what you based this decision on?"

"We'll, um, Roark, it comes down to customer satisfaction," Cusack had thought this would be a painless ten minute meeting. He was visibly flustered in that it wasn't heading down that road.

"Which customer has not been completely satisfied with my work?"

"It's the look, the feel of the company. That's the vision, you see. We need more sales-oriented cost accountants, Roark, more people-oriented."

"What are you saying? You want salesmen for accountants?"

"No, but, um, some of our customers get turned off by—"

"What customers? Who have I possibly turned off?"

"Well," Cusack stumbled awkwardly for an answer, "Steve Barrett said..."

"I've never worked for Barrett. I've never worked his account. I met him once at the Christmas party. Why on earth would you ever talk to Steve Barrett about me?"

Cusack was silent. I knew Steve Barrett to be another of Cusack's college pals. Nice to know I'm mocked by management and client chums alike. So that's what this all boiled down to, some silly popularity contest. I started to laugh. At least I'd managed to, momentarily, wipe that smarmy look off Cusack's face. I'd even surprised myself. In fact, this was probably the most I'd ever said to Cusack in my life, certainly since Pritchard Jr. had decided to give him the keys to the company after Jonathan's funeral. That had been a very dark day. And right now it felt damned good to put Cusack on edge. It was a grand screwing all right, but, as the comedy routine goes, I knew it, and he knew it, and he knew I knew it, and so on and so on...

8

Cusack is the bridge to the Twenty-first Century, all sizzle without the steak, all frosting without the cake. A smooth talker, no problem there. The paradigm, the new paradigm of schmoozers. No trouble whatsoever with people. Not him. I may have the quality, but I lack the sizzle. And, in the grand scheme of things, sizzle is everything.

"What a convergence," I mumbled half-heartedly.

"What?" Cusack broke his silence.

"There was stubble in my wife's bathroom sink when I came home from Atlanta yesterday."

"Huh?" Cusack now looked completely lost.

"You see I never shave there...and now I'm getting fired by a guy who thinks quality is a song, a dance, and a wink, all paperclipped to a billing statement. The cult of the blowhard. I know it's all crunching numbers, Cusack, but it can be art. Doing it right can be goddamned poetry in motion."

My eyes watered up and I wiped them on my sleeve. That's when I noticed the blotch of a shadow spider crawling across his desk. I watched it slowly hover over Cusack's golf-tee paperweight, his stapler and coffee mug, then sail over his keyboard. It didn't matter. I didn't care. A convergence. To come together, to unite. The events of the last couple days, years, life, were converging. And it just didn't matter. What was that childhood game I enjoyed so much? The one where you kept adding straws until they eventually broke the camel's back?

"So you want me out because I don't fit in with your vision, whatever the hell that vision is?" The shadow inched up Cusack's shirt, button by button, passing over his initials, MKC, which he had monogrammed over the pocket of all his tailored dress shirts. "And meanwhile my wife is having someone else shave in her bathroom..."

"Jesus, Roark," Cusack frowned and peeked down at his watch again. This meeting was getting much too strange, running much too late, "Get ahold of yourself, there's certainly nothing that—"

"Why don't you shut-up?!"

The shadow hand clawed inward. Startled, Cusack grabbed at his tie, his collar, his throat. The cold, iron hand began its powerful crush, full of the hate I'd always known was there, and had somehow now unleashed. Cusack began to rise, pulled upward by his neck, as though a hydraulic lift were beneath his chair. Gasping for air, he began to kick awkwardly outward. A terrified foot hit at his monitor, knocked it to the floor with a crashing thud, startling me out of my catatonia.

I ran to Cusack, struggled with the darkness laced around his throat, the ice-black, choking collar wrapping ever tighter, strangling him, turning his face blue, bulging his eyes to the point of popping. I pulled Cusack down, tried to break the cold shadow-grip about his throat. Suddenly several hands grabbed me from behind and forced me to the floor.

But, by that time, Mike Cusack was very dead.

My trial was mercifully brief. Choking your employer to death will get you second-degree in most states. I never told about the shadow. Or about its remarkable power. I didn't want that type of attention. I already had my hands full of the loner-goes-berserk garden variety. I think that *Hard Copy*, *A Current Affair* and *Geraldo* can do quite well without having a segment spotlighting me, thank you very much.

As for my cellmate Webber, he'd been making some rather graphic remarks regarding certain things he had in store for me. The type of things that make it awful hard for a fellow to get much sleep at night. But that's behind me now. The guards all swore I strangled him, then, evidently, leapt back onto the top bunk while he continued to die for another minute or two while they made their futile attempts at first aid.

I'm kept in solitary confinement much of the time now. I don't mind. It's a place where there are no eyes for me to avoid. It's dark here most of the time. Not much light for silly things such as shadows.

Detached. It's a funny word, isn't it? I remember how we would detach the files off e-mail, then toss them onto an Excel spreadsheet. I like the word detach. Much better than perforate or tear off. Or even unleash. Don't you think?

For you see, as Webber lay there, drowning in his own larynx, and as the guards made their meaningless attempts to help, I felt it. A small tug. A wave of emptiness that passed quickly through me. Probably wouldn't have noticed, or put it together, had I not also seen it sliding weightlessly over the backs of the prison guards. My shadow lingered at the edge of the cell for an instant. A final look back at its only friend, a dark nod, before it slipped around the corner and was gone. Its great escape complete.

I wonder how it's doing, what it's doing? But I guess I know. I'm all its known these past lonely years. I'm the only one. Its best friend. An only love in its sea of cold, dark hate. We've shared a strange umbilicus, now broken...

And I can only wonder when they'll bring me the news. The news of what has occurred to a wayward, cheating wife, to a man who shaves where he ought not, to the spoiled cronies busily destroying Jonathan Pritchard's firm, to the other people who've inflicted the thousands of humiliations that a bonefully timid fellow like myself is forced to endure, to endlessly choke down...

But I have a feeling it won't be long in coming.

Eykiltimac Stump Acres

"He's saying it again."

"What?"

"At breakfast today he kept on about Eykiltimac Stump Acres. Said it two or three times and nodded at his companions."

"Doesn't ring a bell," I looked at Jane, the nurse's assistant. What a saint she is, providing the elbow grease necessary to take care of all the lost souls in this the final wing of the assisted care nursing home...the Alzheimer's wing.

"Eykiltimac wasn't a resort you two used to visit? Or perhaps someplace his parents took him when he was a child?"

"There was a Stump Acres south of Fairmont. But it was just several miles of wooded area outside of town."

"Often, at this stage, I've noticed the memories get reshuffled. You know, the earlier ones get placed in front."

"Yes, but I can't recall him ever talking about any 'Eykiltimac.' Hmmm."

I walked into the day room and there he sat. Dwight. My Dwighty. Easy to spot with that distinguished mane of silver hair. Even now I get a little giddy. I watch him from behind for a bit, just pretending he's at home in his worn, old easy chair, just loafing after a long day's work, reading the paper and telling me how delicious the smells are coming from the kitchen. Even when I threw something together on the fly or cooked the roast too long 'til it tasted like leather. He always said something positive.

I love my Dwight. I visit him every day since the harsh reality finally broke through my stubborn collection of little denials and I realized that I just couldn't manage, at seventy-three, to care for him at home anymore. It was, without any doubt, the most painful decision I'd ever made. But you see Dwight started to wander outside whenever I took a bath or got on the phone in a different room. Dwight and I have always loved our walks together. Alone, he'd get disoriented, confused, and frightened. Thank God the neighbors knew, and cared, and helped.

Dwight and I have been married fifty-four years. We celebrated our fifty-fourth anniversary right here in this sitting room. The kids and grandkids were all here for our special day. And it had been a good day for Dwight—with brief recognitions and half conversations. He's deteriorated noticeably since then.

11

But whenever I approach him from behind, like this, I can pause a second or two and let the fantasy bring me back to the fifties, or the sixties, or seventies, or eighties. He still knows me. My name may escape him, but he knows.

Dwight and I are both Fairmont kids. Small town born and bred. Spent our first year of marriage there, too. Although the John Deere sales job took us to the big city, we never changed. Married Dwight the week of my twentieth birthday. He was twenty-two, back from the war, and raring for life, but still hayseed enough to take little old me out for a cherry coke, and a walk around the lake. I knew it was real that very first night Dwight kissed me and told me he could see his future swirling endlessly in the deep blue wells of my eyes. I reckon I saw mine, too. Wouldn't have missed it for all the world.

"Why hello Honey," I came around and took hold of his hand. Always the gentleman, Dwight stood and gave me a peck on the cheek. We sat for awhile, held hands, gave inseparable warmth to each other. I didn't try to force conversation. It wasn't needed and would only verify how far my husband had fallen. But Jane's questions had peeked my curiosity.

"Dwighty," I said and he looked at me. "They say you've been talking about Eykiltimac Stump Acres." Dwight stared at my face. I gave it one more try, "Eykiltimac Stump Acres."

"Ah yes, yes," there was a momentary gleam in his eyes as though I'd whispered his mother's name, a fleeting focus, a kernel of togetherness. "Eykiltimac...Stump Acres."

"What Hon?" I thought I'd heard something confusing, something else. "What did you say?"

But it was gone. Lost in the past. Like all our other days. Dwight continued to nod his head like a guilty schoolboy listening to the headmaster. A habit I'd long recognized as meaning nothing except, perhaps, a fragment of remaining knowledge regarding human interaction.

I sat by my love all day.

I woke with a cold start. Nights were hardest with Dwight no longer here to comfort me after a bad dream. Only this wasn't a dream. It had come to me, slowly, like mist over a lake. I knew it sounded ridiculous. But it was past two in the morning, a time when your mind starts to wander toward places it shouldn't. Places where you think the unthinkable. Thoughts that would be chuckled at in the light of day. Nevertheless I found myself wide awake, frightened, and wandering into one such shadowy place. I realized what Dwight had mumbled this afternoon. It buzzed inside my head like bees about their hive.

I still drive. Did most of it after Dwight's retirement, when we both knew it wouldn't be safe for Dwight to get behind the wheel of the big green Buick anymore. I got in the car without a second thought this morning and decided to put some fresh cut flowers on the graves of my parents, look around, perhaps dig up a memory or two. Getting to Fairmont was a lot easier than it had been in years gone by, ever since they put in the interstate. Cut the time in half.

By two o'clock I found myself at the Fairmont library. The librarian—she was a new face, but then I'd been away for so many years they were all new to me—she showed me where the microfiche from the Fairmont Tribunes were kept. I'd worked at Fairmont's library myself over half a century ago. Much different back then, back before they'd moved to the new building, which by now was far from new also. You could see how the wood was cracked, dry rotting around the windows. There was a light smell of mold. All things age.

Stump Acres was densely wooded, an area used mostly by hunters during deer season. It had, in fact, been at Stump Acres where an old childhood chum of mine, Craig Muntean, had been accidentally shot and killed by one of his hunting mates years and years ago. That was in the days before the hunters started wearing those big orange parkas for all the others to see.

Truth be known, Craig had been my first boyfriend from way back in early school. The Muntean family had been shattered at the loss of their only son. It had been a tragedy all around. I know we hadn't been five years out of high school when I'd heard about Craig's unfortunate death. Dwight and I were only in our first years of marriage. My little Joey had just been born when I'd heard the news. With that timeframe in mind I began my search.

It didn't take as long as I'd thought. The Tribune only came out twice weekly back then, perhaps it still does. There it was. **Fairmont Man Dies in Hunting Accident**. Good grief. Poor Craig. Never given a chance to live, to flourish, to love. I read the detailed article and wiped away the tears with my sleeve.

It turned out that the authorities never found out which other hunter had shot Craig. It was most likely a stray bullet that had traveled some distance before finding a new home in Craig's lung. Or perhaps the hunter knew what he'd done, had seen it up close, panicked, and was too afraid to come forward. Fairmont is a small community, and something like that would've been hard to live with. Very hard.

13

A few minutes out of Fairmont, I pulled the green Buick over to the side of Interstate 90, closed my eyes and rubbed at my temples. It was ludicrous for me to even think such nonsense. I should be ashamed of myself. Dwight had simply muttered something incoherent after I'd mentioned what the nurse's aide had said. Dwight just parroted back some disjointed syllables. That's all it had been. Nothing more.

I turned the Buick around and headed back. Took a room at the Holiday Inn. When Dwight and I first met, I had been lightly dating a gentleman named Pete Henderson. Pete had been the summer lifeguard at Sisseton Lake. He had been a young man who'd just finished his first year of studies at the University, but he spent his summers in Fairmont giving swimming lessons and watching over the crowd of people frolicking at the local beach.

Pete's brother Harlan had married my high school girlfriend's sister, Gwen Wharton. It had given us a basis to strike up a conversation. Pete was certainly a bronzed Adonis, tall and sharply muscular, a great swimmer—like Johnny Weismuller, and that's why everyone nicknamed him Tarzan. But, unfortunately, Pete was also as dull as yesterday's dishwater. He loved swimming, had won numerous championships in high school, and didn't really talk about much else. We were never more than casual friends who caught a handful of movies together. Pete had fallen quietly by the wayside as soon as I'd met Dwight.

There was only one Wharton phone number in the Fairmont phonebook, the slim phone directory sitting on the table in my suite. I didn't know quite what to say. I knew Loretta had moved to California eons ago, right after her marriage. After a decade of Christmas cards, we'd eventually lost touch. I felt awkward, but I dialed the number.

"Hello." It was a woman's voice. She sounded middle-aged.

"Uh hi," I almost hung up. "My name is Ann-Marie Warner. I grew up with a Loretta Wharton and I was wondering if—"

"Oh yes, Aunt Loretta."

"Superb, I was afraid I didn't have the correct number."

"We're the only Wharton's left in Fairmont. Would you like Loretta's number? She lives in California."

"Loretta's still there, huh? I'm kind of embarrassed but the last time I saw Loretta was at her wedding."

"Oh boy, I guess you haven't been in touch with Aunt Loretta in quite a while then?"

"We kind of lost touch over the years. I've been trying to look up some old Fairmont girlfriends of mine."

"Let me get you her phone number."

14

"That would be great," I said, then took the plunge. "Say, how are Gwen and Harlan?"

"You knew them, too?"

"I sure did. Gwen was so pretty. We all wanted to look just like her. Loretta and I were a few years younger, but Gwen would let us play with her makeup."

"Goodness sakes. Well now Harlan passed away awhile back. Cancer. Gwen lives in the Cities near her kids."

"I'm sorry to hear about Harlan. Come to think of it, I also knew Harlan's brother Pete." I squeezed the phone tightly, "Would you happen to know how he's doing?"

"Oh girl, you have been away a long while. Pete died before I was born. He drowned in Lake Sisseton."

According to Loretta's niece, lifeguard Pete Henderson had drowned in Lake Sisseton one summer night. Some kids, out later than their parents would have liked, found Pete's lifeless body bobbing and floating near the dock. My swimming Adonis, the local Tarzan, and championship lifeguard, had drowned in less than four feet of water.

This morning I'd traveled from Fairmont to Mankato. For you see there was only one other man who'd ever been in my life, however insignificantly, peripherally. I remember that warm June night on the picnic blanket in the park when Dwight and I had confided our past romances to one another. Over fifty years ago, but now clear as yesterday. It was the sort of talk that lovers have as they share past secrets and other such silliness with one another. I'd confessed to Dwight of having had a secret crush on my freshman English teacher at Mankato State University. Professor Applegate—with his bushel of strawberry blond curls and horn-rim glasses—had been so young, so poetic, barely out of college himself. It was a silly school girl's crush that had amounted to nothing beyond signing up for all of his courses. But I'd laughingly shared that with Dwight.

At the Mankato State Alumni Office, I dug through shelves of musty yearbooks as they forged ever onward after my years there, half a century before. Every year held another picture of a slightly more worn, more ruffled Professor Applegate. About fifteen yearbooks passed before I came across the dedication. It was in the 1961 yearbook, on the very last page.

The dedication was to Mankato State's Professor Applegate who had died earlier that semester. At the bottom of this full page picture of the professor read a brief passage from Hamlet: *"Good night, sweet Prince, And flights of angels sing thee to thy rest."* Beneath that quotation, in smaller

15

font, were the dates of his birth and untimely death. Unfortunately, nothing in the yearbook alluded as to how the late Professor had passed away.

Of late I'd become an unlikely expert at culling through old newspapers on file. The reason it took longer than expected was the feeling of dread, of me putting off the inevitable, of not wanting to confront the unthinkable. I delayed for hours over coffee before going to the local library. But by the early afternoon I had it all laid out in front of me. The police would have tossed it up to a simple hit and run, possibly some damn fool driving drunk, except for one small fact. The evidence at the scene pointed out how the car that ran down Professor Applegate on that dark, deserted street had then stopped, backed up, and run over him again. And again. And again.

In those days John Deere had Dwight doing all that tri-state traveling he'd hated so much. Kept him away from me, he'd always say. And I remember one particularly dark night when he came home after midnight. The kids were asleep. Dwight apologized endlessly for being late, and for causing me any undue worry which was the last thing he'd ever want, but, he told me, he'd hit an enormous deer that had jumped onto the road from out of nowhere. The Hudson, Dwight had informed me, was one hellish mess, just leave it for him to clean up. He spent most of the next two days alone in the garage, scrubbing gristle off the grill, pounding out the dents, replacing a headlamp and both front tires. Then adding a touch of paint here and there.

I sit here next to Dwight and hold his hand. How many millions of times have I held this hand. I find everything quite impossible to believe. Delusions of a silly old woman approaching senility herself. Craig was simply killed in a hunting accident. A drunken, failing student had most likely killed Professor Applegate. Pete Henderson lived to swim and, unfortunately, drowned as a result of his lifelong passion.

In the course of my long years, I don't know why any of these events should have seemed sinister or connected. I've seen too many strange things unfold daily on TV and in the newspaper. I'm ashamed of myself for taking it all to such a ridiculous extreme. The whole thing is more a reflection of me than Dwight. But, even now, in the cool light of day, the doubts linger and dance. Insistently. In the back of my mind. I find myself transfixed by Dwight's profile.

"Dwight, dear," I whisper and softly kiss my husband's cheek. "Do you remember Pete Henderson? You know, the lifeguard from Fairmont. The one I dated, briefly, before we met."

Dwight stares at me. His eyes are glazed and dull as they search my face. It was as though he could sense something important but couldn't quite connect, couldn't quite understand.

"Pete Henderson, you remember, the big lifeguard at Sisseton." The questioning soon became too painful, too wrenching to continue. I leaned over and gave Dwight a hug, wanting to pull his warmth into me, wanting so desperately to squeeze back the past.

"I-killed-im-at the lake..."

"What Dwighty?" I looked up. "What did you just say?"

But Dwight's eyes were now unfocused, dim. He began to nod his head like one of those tilting-bird paperweights the children play with.

Oh dear Dwighty. Dear sweet Dwighty. You know you've always been my knight in shinning armor. I've always thought of you in that mythical manner. Right from the very first. I love you so much, Dwight. Always have. Always will. And I've always known that you've loved me too. Its been obvious throughout our many, many years together.

But until now, until right this very moment ... I just never knew how much.

Blue Mist

A swirl of fine blue mist. Free-falling like a carnival ride.

It's an eerie dream - haunting, foreboding. I suddenly find myself in a phone booth. I look out, it's dark, but I see Lisa-Marie in the car, for some reason I look at my watch, someone, I'm not sure who, but someone I should know, is calling my name, over and over again, and Lisa is running toward me, eyes wide with panic and fright.

Too much TV, I guess. Or spicy food. More likely the daily news. The Slicer has certainly placed our town on the map. At first he didn't make much of a ripple as the early victims were homeless, what we called vagrants or bums in an earlier age. The initial fatalities were discovered in their cardboard boxes or underpass shelters east of the railroad tracks, near the base of Knot Hill, their throats cut from ear to ear. The police wrote the first couple off as some internal turf war among the dregs of society - likely a lethal squabble over a bottle of Schnapps. Bottom feeders killing each other, who cared? The perp, some brain-fried wino, probably hopped a train and by now was five-hundred miles away, no doubt panhandling in Chicago.

After the third homicide, the police started to worry, did the legwork, scoured the surroundings for clues, interviewed potential witnesses - the works. Although professing to be following up on several hot leads, no arrests had been made. But sections of the first autopsy report were leaked to the press. The killer had been sloppy, rushed in his first taste of blood, and a minuscule piece from the tip of the blade had broken off and lodged in the victim's spinal column at the back of the throat. Detectives speculated, based upon this piece of evidence, and the sharpness and depth of the cuts, that the killer was using a large Butterfly knife, one of those razor-sharp slicers with the flipping blade, like those seen in the old Bruce Lee movies.

The Knot Hill Guardian printed the nickname being quietly whispered amongst the trash-can fires in the transient community - and the legend of the "Knot Hill Slicer" was born. The name stuck, even when the Slicer moved his act uptown.

Blue mist. Free-fall. Lisa-Marie. Sweet, beautiful Lisa-Marie.
Someone…is…coming.

Alice Cora Hailey Blackstone, recently widowed, and the last living descendant of the Hailey Canning Factory, had been spending her twilight years performing philanthropic deeds for the city that had, since the turn of the last century, made the Hailey clan exceptionally wealthy. Recent charities included a grant to restore the opera house to its original condition, donations of new computers to the City Library, and an endowment to set up a summer camp for underprivileged children. An early morning jogger, hearing yelps from what he believed to be a puppy in distress, cut down an alley off Chestnut Street, mere blocks from town square. The jogger found a poodle struggling against a leash clenched tightly in Mrs. Hailey's rigor-mortised fist. She was lying in a crimson pillow of her own blood, marble eyes begging someone to take care of her pet.

Then a young father by the name of Phil Warner had gone to the all-night grocery on 7th and James - not even a half mile from the church where Lisa-Marie and I were wed - to pick up an emergency bundle of Pampers. Hours later, alerted to his absence by a panicky Mrs. Warner, the police found him in his Ford at the edge of the parking lot, head hunched over the steering wheel, warm blood still dripping onto his lap.

Another woman was found in the wooded part of the bike track that circles Gomsrud lake. Days later a postman was found in the lobby of a brownstone tenement near the warehouse district, his bag of mail lying next to him, undelivered. Most recently a retired couple, Ben and Hazel Jenkins, passing through Knott Hill on their way to Arizona, were found at the KOA campgrounds south of town - bled dry in their own Airstream camper.

The Knot Hill Slicer certainly cast a pall over this old berg. Restaurants closing early, late shows at the theaters canceled, police escorts available - and the FBI was lending a hand. The national news and the cables' surfeit of true-crime freak shows have Knott Hill squarely in their cross-hairs; interviewing family members of the deceased with such sympathetic eyes, itemizing every gory detail for the viewers while feigning humanity - then creaming their knickers hustling to get their stories on the air, and snarfing down a few bar drinks, while secretly hoping that the Slicer ups the ante. The authorities are bound to catch up with him - just a matter of time...and victims.

Blue mist. Lisa-Marie sits waiting in the car. Someone calls my name.

I'm here again, repeatedly, loop-to-loop, caught in the same dream night after night. What's...going...on?

I push away my thoughts, exile the floating sensation. As always I think of Lisa-Marie. When did we last kiss? Hold hands? Make love? Why don't I know? I'm lost inside a dream. I will wake up. And Lisa-Marie will be there.

19

Lisa-Marie…will…be…there.

Free-falling through blue mist. A fine blue mist. Where are my days?
Lisa-Marie sits alone in the car. My god, oh dear god, she's crying.
A phone booth - casket-like - awaits.
Realization…Blue mist.

The mist vanishes, and I'm left with an epiphany. The sudden clarity of it all breaks my heart as I feel Lisa-Marie's sobs of grief. Her tears are for me.

For you see, it's not my dream I find myself trapped in…It's his.

Obsolete realities float away like fog over a lake. The only thing professing the truth, telling me what I once was, is Lisa-Marie's love; bike rides at dusk, the strawberry-honey smell of her black hair, our first date where we left the dance and went fishing, tux, gown and all, the deep-brown eyes that believed in me even when I had self-doubts, the way she looked from our first born and back to me that winter night when our daughter came weeks early. An indescribable connection with Lisa-Marie - symbiotic - as she lies weeping; an ethereal bearing perhaps called devotion.

Gerald Davitt, VP at Klondeen Software, and his wife, recently empty nested, had bought a condo in the well-to-do section of the city, and were having a gathering. By the time the sitter arrived we were running a half-hour late. Idiot me left Gerald's directions at the office, and was winging it in the true male tradition. Idiot me had been meaning to recharge the battery in my cell phone for days, but never got around to it. Idiot me left my beautiful wife, one last caress of her cheek with my fingertips, to call Gerald from a corner phone booth. Idiot me jotting down choppy directions from Gerald. Idiot me looking at the un-bathed young man with the Trotsky goatee and black wool hat rolled down over his ears. Idiot me believing that the Knot Hill Slicer truly wanted to know what time it was. Idiot me looking up from my watch to see that he's got something sharp and shiny in his hand. Idiot me too confused to react till I see his back hastily dashing away. Idiot me turning toward the car, seeing blood, mine, on the glass partition of the booth. Idiot me sliding to the ground, holding my throat with one hand, as Lisa-Marie rushes toward me, and Gerald keeps repeating, somewhere, off in the darkness, "Aaron? Aaron? Are you there? Aaron?"

And idiot me, lying there on the cold pavement, dying in my love's arms.

Denial…Acceptance…Blue mist.

20

Where do I go when he's not asleep? Lost in a swirl of past realities, frozen inside a dark mirror, an apparition of fleeting consciousness, I haunt his dreams. A perverted twist on Descartes' assertion - *I'm in the Knot Hill Slicer's nightmare, therefore I am...*

I walk my plank toward the phone booth, dial Gerald's number, and await my murder. But I'm sentient, lucid in another's dream. I hear the footsteps behind me. I now understand the pause as he scopes out his prey. He approaches. Perhaps, with perception, there can be a shifting of events - a changing.

I hang up on Gerald and turn to greet the Knot Hill Slicer.

Hey, Mister - you got the time?

Though the black wool hat works as a disguise, I see the three silver rings pierced into the side of his right eyebrow. His skin is pale, acne-scarred, the scrawny bag-of-bones can't weigh more than one-thirty soaking wet. *This goddamned dream,* I read in his eyes, *this goddamned dream again.*

The Knot Hill Slicer pulls the blade, the Butterfly knife that's served him so well in this, his season of awakening. The blade flashes across my line of sight. I catch his wrist on the opposite side, blood on the knife, blood spraying onto his jacket and goatee'd chin.

You're done. My voice comes out in low gurgles. I squish his hand in mine. He struggles to free himself of my grip. I clutch his throat with my free hand and push him against the brick wall. Somehow I know his name. *All done now, Edgar.*

He struggles in the dream, his nightmare, and fights to wake. But I'm holding him, and have his wrist, forcing it upward, the tip of his blade now scratching his silver eyebrow rings. We look deep into each other's eyes, and I feel his midnight battle, his screaming silent plea: *Wake, for god's sake, wake up, please, wake now.*

My right hand digs into his throat. I feel the Slicer shaking, the violent convulsions of a fish caught on a line, twisted up in greasy bedsheets, and thrashing raggedly as he battles for the safety of consciousness. I hang on to his throat, the spot he's found so very endearing, not letting him go, feeling the heartbeat with each of his struggling kicks toward daylight, and the world in which he is never the victim.

Why you!? I hear his final thoughts. *How can this be happening!?*

I turn his head toward me with the tip of his own blade, forcing the Knot Hill Slicer to witness his future in the deep blue mist of my eyes...death, its ownself. I feel him screaming, mouth wide open in the day world, but eyes shut as the rest of him remains in mine. As though crushing a wren in the palm of my hand, I feel his heart beat ebb. Let the neighbors hear the ruckus and call the police, let the authorities find him, find his Butterfly knife, find the clippings I know he worships, and let them know it's over.

All done now, Edgar.

I feel the Slicer's heart stop, his features now still, etched in ice in both our worlds. I release my grip. Something tells me we'll be getting off at different stops.

The blue mist washes over me. And through the mist I see Lisa-Marie. She's sleeping. Dried tears line her eyes. And though I now have no hands, I caress Ann's face with my fingertips. Sapphire droplets dance on her cheek. The blue mist washes over me…and I wonder what lies next.

Lisa-Marie wakes to daylight shining through the curtains. Ann can't believe she slept this late, this soundly. The exhaustion from the last few weeks have caught up with her. She remembers having a pleasant dream. Aaron was there. She felt him in her heart, where he'll always be.

But today's another day, and she must be strong for the children. Lisa-Marie turns on the local news where a late story is breaking…

Per Diem

I despise business travel. Always have. Usually I sit back on my Corporate perch, crunch the numbers, count the beans and toss in my two cents. But Gipps felt that a flowery show of all four of us senior partners might give the Screen-Com execs that extra nudge needed to have them switch over to our software. And Gipps' instincts for closing a sale are a proven commodity at Corporate. We'd been lucky to scarf him up from Apple.

Although my suite at the Seattle Sheraton was first-class, I didn't get much sleep. I never do sleep well in strange places. The airline food gave me heartburn and I lay awake most of the night staring up at the ceiling.

After our breakfast, break-the-ice meeting with the Screen-Com group, I realized that I'd left my laptop back on the night table in my room. I excused myself and headed back to fetch it. I was already weary and it had the definite makings of a long day. I popped a Tums.

When the elevator doors opened on the ninth floor, my floor, I had to jerk sideways in order to avoid a sharp collision with a team of paramedics wheeling a blanketed figure atop a collapsible gurney. I slid out of the elevator while keeping the door from shutting in order to let them board. I couldn't help but notice the soaking black hair, long and snarled, dangling out from under the white blanket and draping floorwards over the side of the gurney. Droplets of water flicked with every bump or quick move and rained onto the carpeted floor. The elevator doors slid shut on the paramedic team and their lifeless cargo.

People were milling about the hallway, whispering excitedly. I was able to gather from the snippets of conversation that the woman had drowned in her bathtub. Heading toward my suite I passed a tall policeman standing in front of what I assumed to be her room. Other uniforms and hotel officials appeared to be talking inside. I popped another Tums into my mouth.

The Sheraton did a great job at damage control. During lunch I was paged by the concierge, taken to a plush office in back, and had the awkward events from upstairs calmly explained to me. The poor woman had spent a great deal of the previous evening drinking cocktails in the hotel bar, as business travelers are oft to do. The bartender remembers her leaving alone. She returned to her room, ran a brimming tubfull of hot water for a bath and, evidently, had been so intoxicated that she passed out, slipped down and drowned.

The police, the concierge firmly assured me, had found no signs of foul play whatsoever. No struggle. No burglary. Nothing missing. The poor woman had missed a breakfast appointment and, when she didn't answer her phone, some concerned colleagues came up to check. The door was locked. No one answered their repeated knocks. Her colleagues grew more alarmed, got a hold of the front desk, who immediately sent up a bell-boy to open the door and...

Lord how I despise business travel.

The Seattle trip to meet the Screen-Com execs was my last business trip. Gipps, as usual, had keen instincts and we won over the software account. That happened one year ago this past month.

Everyone needs a release valve...Don't they?

Mine is the StairMaster. Forty minutes a night. Or thirty. Or twenty. I used to jog back when that was vogue. Might even find an old pair of Nikes stuffed in a drawer somewhere if I were to look. Some might enjoy sports, theater, reading. Perhaps womanizing. Maybe even gambling. Others turn to the bottle. Whatever. I'm a StairMaster man myself.

Eugene Gipps has been our top salesman for the ninth year in a row. Corporate's market share, under Gipps' personal tutelage, has tripled in the past five years alone. Gipps has made us all very comfortable financially. Corporate's been good to him too.

Gipps is a selling machine. He keeps a penthouse apartment in the city, but can't live there more than three, maybe four weeks a year tops. Gipps lives in the field. The man's true homes are the nation's Hyatt's, Sheraton's, Embassy Suites, or The Fairmont's and Hiltons of Chicago, Seattle, San Francisco, Houston, Los Angeles and New York. Gipps' schedule would drive me nuts. No downtime to recharge the battery, no breathing room, no quiet. Always out rubbing elbows with clients, making sure they were happy, wining and dining them into long term business contracts. I don't know how he stands it. No sports, movies, gambling, or women. It's worrisome. His existence is different places, overly rich food, living in taxis, endless lobbies and crowded airports. Who could possibly enjoy that? We don't push him. Lately we've tried to settle him down. He doesn't seem close to burnout, but we worry.

"Gene," I recall saying to Gipps a dozen times, "Bootsie and I want you up at the lake cabin for the long weekend."

"No can do Tim." Gipps' always had a flight to catch, "Got to be in Dallas Monday AM for the Trade Show."

I usually get a large packet of his travel expenditures whenever he's in town. Gipps informally chucks everything into a manila envelope and

24

drops it on my secretary's desk whenever he pops by the office. With a life spent on the road you can image how stuffed and disordered Eugene's envelope often gets. We have proper forms for business travel that all other employees must fill out or face an irate me. But with Gipps, I let it fly. When a man spends his life making you a millionaire, you don't screw him with protocol. There was no way I'd force our standard bureaucracy on Eugene. He's too busy bringing home the bacon to dot the I's and cross all T's. Gipps is a dynamo. Always on the go, always wining, dining, elbow-rubbing, always ready and on key. Eugene lives on the corporate credit card, and we say more power to him.

I handle Gipps' travel expense personally. I make sense of all his loose threads, the entire morass of vouchers, receipts and invoices. I'm a very good accountant. If the auditors or any IRS boys should stop by, unexpected, I'll lean back in my chair, put my feet up on the cherrywood, grin at them, and with a good conscience tell them to wake me up when they're done. Everything gets reconciled, always does, one column or another.

Gipps dropped off his Chicago travel expenses for the previous week's regional sales conference this morning. Then he was straight off to New York for more negotiations with the Monitrom folks. I shuffled through the packet of invoices randomly stuffed in an envelope and chuckled.

I couldn't find Gipps' back-up for the Hyatt Regency. Oh well. Details. I had my secretary ring up the bookkeepers at the Hyatt Chicago on Wacker Street and patch me through to an operator who could fax me a printout of Gipps' Hyatt invoice which I needed for our pristine records.

"Oh gosh, he was here on Wednesday when...." the voice on the other end stuttered after I read off the dates of Gipps' stay. "Did Mr. Gipps tell you about the incident?" asked the older women's trembling voice.

"What incident?"

"I'm not really supposed to say anything about it. But your employee had to have heard. It's practically all that's been on the news this past week."

I could tell that it was just eating her up to gab about this incident, this something out of the norm, and she'd definitely piqued my interest. I gave it the extra push, "Mr. Gipps was in and out, and we didn't have a chance to chat. What happened?"

"Well, they really don't want us to talk about the incident. But Channel 13 says they're going to arrest her husband pretty soon so it won't hurt to..."

I listened as she worked her way through the story. The Hyatt bookkeeper told me how one of their maids had been found dead last week in the room she had been cleaning. She'd been strangled with the curtain cord which, left tied about her throat, had kept her swaying in some warped, slow dance macabre right in front of the window, her bulging eyes staring blindly out over Lake Michigan.

The maid was discovered when a family, who'd come to visit Chicago from rural Wisconsin so that their kids could see Shedd's Aquarium, checked into the room for the surprise of their lives. It was obviously her husband, the woman told me earnestly, after all they'd been having arguments ever since he'd lost his job at the shipyard.

Toward the end I started taking notes. When I hung up, I realized that I'd never given her my fax number. But by then I was on to reconciling something altogether different. Something that gnawed lightly in the back of my consciousness. A fleeting thought. A thought that returned, stronger and purposeful.

I'm a cost accountant at heart, by choice and by profession. I had all the tools right there in front of me. The expense reports were at my fingertips. I had all of the exact dates and cities. I could tap into the Internet and do a website search of the different newspapers from the different cities. I'd work it for a few minutes, maybe a half-hour, tops.

Funny how time flies when you get involved. I shut my eyes. The strain from staring at the monitor all day has left me with a migraine. I'd better call Bootsie and tell her to keep my half in the oven. But I don't think I'll tell her what I've been working on for the past eight hours. No, I don't think I will.

Going back an arbitrary year and a half, I decided to plot out each one in detail. The records nerd in me, I guess. I told my secretary to stay late, had her find me a current map of downtown Houston in order to help me locate the first one. Yup. There it was. Two blocks down from the Ritz.

The Houston Post article told how the woman had left the Italian restaurant, alone, that evening and walked to the ramp in which she'd parked her car. She was found the next morning, sitting in front of the steering wheel, with the shoulder strap of her seat belt wound tightly around her throat. Her larynx was crushed. The expense report, yanked from the archive, showed that Gipps had eaten dinner at the same restaurant that very evening. It was odd in that Gipps' dinner receipt indicated that he'd paid for this particular outing with cash. How...unlike him.

The San Francisco Chronicle told a similar story. A business woman had been returning to the Fairmont Hotel, after an evening of browsing in Union Square, when she'd been grabbed from behind, dragged into a dark alley, and choked to death with the strap of her own purse. Her body was then stuffed into a dumpster. Eugene had made several profitable leads at that

San Fran Tech Show where he stayed four days at the Fairmont that very same week.

At the Hotel Sofetel in Minneapolis, which coincided with Gipps' conference with the Honeywell Group, a female chefette, who worked the coffee shop's lonely overnight shift, was found in the meat freezer, strangled with her own apron.

At the Los Angeles Hilton, during a NewTech sponsored lobbyist convention, the one that Gipps had spearheaded, there had been another drowning, much like the one last year in Seattle. It had been ruled an accident. No foul play. No robbery. The door had been locked. But then again, how much does it take to clean up a one-sided struggle in a hotel bathroom, then let the door latch lock shut as you slip silently out into a midnight hallway?

At New York City's Emerald Plaza Hotel, coinciding with Gipps' signing of the Hexcon Industries account, a cocktail waitress left for a quick break to call her boyfriend and never returned. Janitors found her early the next morning in a desolate, downstairs hallway. Her body was stuffed inside one of those old fashioned, wooden phonebooths. She'd been strangled with the phone cord.

And the list went on...All in all there was a trail of seventeen incidents in eighteen months. Seventeen incidents of Gipps being in the same city, and the immediate vicinity, of the reported events.

I've sat here for hours wondering what makes a man like Eugene Gipps tick. Sleeping in strange places every night, different, endless clients to razzle-dazzle, delayed flights, smoky cab rides, lost luggage, cold room service meals, a mountainous workload. Always on the run. No family. No hobbies. I've always wondered how Gipps did it. How he does it all so well—so effortlessly. And now, dear God, I think I know.

I stare at my notes and contemplate the alternatives. None are too terribly appealing. Confront Eugene? Go to the police? Corporate will go bankrupt with civil suits and bad press. Wait until the media smells the red meat. Not necessarily the cover of *Businessweek* we'd have hoped for. Clients will drop like flies. There's no spin we could put on it that would have a snowball's chance.

...Yet there is another option.

The big three automakers build motorcars knowing the human cost that's paid each week on the highways. How about the alcohol industry? Or tobacco? In the largest sense it's all just another factor in the cost of doing business. Just another capital expenditure like the costs of raw materials or overhead. Or labor or fringies. Or even of one Eugene Gipps' per diem.

After all, everyone needs a release valve.....Don't they?

Free Toy Inside

Kevin marched submissively down the market aisle, listened carefully as his parents discussed the grocery trip, turned his head back and forth, from shelf to shelf, in search of that just-right box of cereal. His parents had promised him that he could choose just one box for himself.

"Take that out of your mouth Wendy," Kevin's dad directed towards Kevin's one-year-old sister. "Jeez, this kid eats everything."

"She's teething," Kevin's mother said. "Maybe that will teach you to give her the shopping list."

Kevin tuned them out and continued his quest. Captain Crunch? No, Kevin had eaten too much of the air-filled Captain lately. Lucky Charms? Frosted Flakes? Trix? Childish stuff. Too boring for a kid who's eight-going-on-nine.

"Dad," Kevin looked up at his father, "can we go to the zoo tomorrow? Billy's parents are taking him and...."

"Sorry, Kev." Kevin's father had finally wrested the half-eaten shopping list away from Wendy's tiny clutches. "Dad'll be darned lucky if he doesn't have to go into the office on Sunday. Why don't you ask your mother?"

"She won't take me." Kevin had already pursued that particular avenue.

"Hurry up and make your pick, Kev." Kevin's father was becoming impatient. "We've got to get this show on the road."

Kevin turned his full attention toward the breakfast foods. Golden Crunch? Malt-O-Meal? Coco Puffs? Kevin had eaten them all before. He was in the mood for something new, something different. Something...Special. Raisin Bran? Froot Loops? Two more big no's. Magic Wishies...? Now what on earth were Magic Wishies?

There was only one box of Magic Wishies left on the shelf. Kevin walked toward the cereal box and stared at the cover. Hmmm. He picked up the package and studied the colorful artwork. The drawing was a simple caricature of a magician squinting outward. Eyes, eyebrows, a hand and a wand made up the entire visual. How lame, Kevin thought as he flipped the lonely carton back on the shelf. How incredibly lame.

It must have been the lighting in the grocery store or, perhaps, the haphazard manner in which he'd tossed the cereal carton back onto the shelf, but as Kevin began to walk away, the box appeared to tilt, almost bend, outward in his direction. And more, the eyes of the etched magician followed his every move. What in heck...?

Oh, I get it, Kevin thought as he went back and reexamined the package of Magic Wishies. The magician was drawn in such a manner that no matter what angle you looked at him, his eyes would follow you. Kevin studied the carton with renewed interest.

Free Toy Inside, a diagonal sentence in the lower left corner of the cereal box screamed out at him. **Make One Wish Come True With Your Magic Wishies' Magic Card** proclaimed the message below the screaming diagonal. Why not, thought Kevin, at least I'll get a free toy.

"Dad," Kevin held the breakfast package toward his father, "I want to pick Magic Wishies. Please Dad, can I pick Magic Wishies!?"

"Yea, sure Kev," Kevin's father was struggling to decipher the moist remnants of the shopping list. "Toss it in the cart."

Later, at the checkout lane, the cashier had trouble scanning the bar code on the cereal package. Over Kevin's assertions that this was the last box, the cashier sent a pimply stock boy back to search the cereal shelves.

"Nice pick, son." Kevin's mother glared impatiently at the cash register.

After what seemed an eternity, with an ever-lengthening line behind them, the stock boy came back shaking his head. The boy also informed them that he didn't have a recollection of ever stocking that particular brand.

"Well, since we can't seem to find the correct price anywhere," the cashier smiled, "it's on us. No charge, sir. That's store policy in situations like these. Sorry about the delay."

Yuck. The Magic Wishies were awful. Not sweet at all. Kevin had so looked forward to trying them when he woke up that morning. Kevin almost spit out the first mouthful, but choked them down. Although shaped like happy-faced stars, the Magic Wishies tasted more like soggy cardboard, with a strange coppery aftertaste. Dad's grocery list had probably tasted better. Cripes, how could a company dare sell such crud?

Kevin tossed in another mouthful, just to confirm their staleness before he discarded the box of Magic Wishies in the kitchen garbage. Hmmm. Not as bad as the first taste. Not nearly. A little crisper, but certainly a metallic aftertaste. Kevin grabbed another fistful. Then, absentmindedly, another. A sudden feeling overtook him, an etching in the back of his mind. What was it? He squinted his eyes, and crunched on more of the cereal. An idea, but much more than that...A bursting kaleidoscope of thoughts exploded in his brain, new thoughts...And something else...Something not quite so pleasant lurking in the shadows.

29

"Ouch!" Kevin dropped the box and looked at his hand. There was a tiny drop of blood on his little finger. What in heck stung me? Kevin stuck his pinky into his mouth and looked down at the package of Magic Wishies. It lay on the floor, almost empty. Great, now mom's gonna kill me when she finds out I ate it all in one sitting. I must have kept shoveling it in without thinking. The cheap junk was mostly air, anyway. Kevin saw that the free toy had fallen out of the box. It was a thin package, about the size of one of his father's plastic credit cards. Oh, Kevin took his pinky out of his mouth, that's what it was—those paper cuts sure do smart. He grabbed the toy off the floor and went back to the table. Kevin tore off the white wrapper and stared at a shiny red tab of paper the size of a baseball card.

"Dad, the free toy inside is a blank baseball card. How chintzy can you get?"

"There are no free toys, Kev." Dad wrinkled his nose as he stood at the sink and rinsed the saliva off of Wendy's teething ring. "No free lunches either. No freebies. Consider it a life lesson, Son. Took me most of thirty-five years to learn that particular one."

Kevin turned the card over in his hand. On the back was a thin, pencil-like drawing of the magician that had been on the cereal carton's cover. The magician even had the same eyes which followed your every move. Below the drawing it read in bold *Hold Card, Close Eyes, and Make Your Magic Wish*. *Only One Wish per Card* read the fine print below. Kevin looked at the card, not quite sure what to make of it.

"Kevin," his mother took the stairs two at a time. She was not a happy camper. "How many times this morning have I told you to clean up your room? Three times today and it's still a mess."

"I was just about to do it."

"You bet you're going to clean it right now, young man." Kevin's mother noticed the box of Magic Wishies lying on the floor. "Why is this on the floor?"

"I'm sorry, Mom. I'll throw it out right now."

But Kevin's mother picked it up, then stared at Kevin, "Young man, I can't believe you ate this entire box." She held her thumb and forefinger an inch apart, "I tell you, Kevin, I am this close to grounding you for a week."

Kevin looked at his mother for several seconds, then across the room at his preoccupied father for several more. Kevin turned the card over, took a big breath, closed his eyes, and ran his tongue across his teeth. The coppery aftertaste lingered in his mouth one final second.

"Kevin," mother said sternly, "you will look at me when I'm talking to you. Do you hear me, young man? And what's that you have in your hands?"

30

Kevin's mother snatched the Magic Wishie card from between his fingers. Kevin opened his eyes and gazed up at his mother.

"Now what on earth have you got here, Kevin?" Kevin's mother stared down at the card, "What does this mean?" His mother's face gradually changed from a light shade of anger to a dark hue of perplexity. "Oh dear God, Kevin, what does this mean? Kevin! Tell me what this means!?"

Something in her tone, the one tone that Kevin's docile father hadn't quite succeeded over the years in filtering out, told him that something was wrong. Something was very wrong. Kevin's father rushed over and looked down at the card his wife held in her trembling hands.

It would be impossible for Kevin to explain what happened next. The only thing he could liken it to was a blip in a movie. The kind of jump you see at the dollar theater where they show second run films that are already beat up and scratchy. Some of those movies have a quick edit where the film may have broken or burned, yet was pieced back together with a frame or two missing. Only this, Kevin thought, was not a movie. This was a blip in real life.

"Hey son," Kevin's father smiled broadly, "you better pack up, that is if you still want to go to the zoo, today. Then how about catching that new Arnold Schwarzenegger movie tonight?"

"You know Kevin," the forgotten card slipped from between mother's fingers and floated leisurely to the kitchen floor, "I think I'll take care of your room myself from now on. What say I have blueberry pancakes waiting for you and Daddy, Kev, when you two get home for dinner?"

Kevin nodded slowly, and when his parents hustled about the business of getting ready for the zoo trip, he retrieved the card from the floor. The piece of paper was now mildly tacky, like cheap fly paper left out too long. The magician's eyes no longer stared back at him. The sentence about making a magic wish was now gone, as though it had never existed. Kevin turned the card over and examined the front.

The image now filling up the previously blank space was in dull colors, almost sepia tones. Like a Polaroid snapshot on bad film. An image of his mother and father, confusion and alarm on their faces. Kevin sensed movement before he actually saw any. This depiction of his parents, their eyes bulging wide in panic, was moving—they were slowly mouthing silent words, staring at Kevin from their tiny, two-dimensional, sepia-colored world, as if a motion picture were itself being run in ultra-slow motion. Kevin watched the excruciatingly sluggish manner in which his miniature parents brought their hands up to their faces in complete shock and terror.

Kevin then watched as his new and improved parents fluttered about the house, serf-like, getting things prepared. Prepared especially for him.

Getting ready for Kevin's big day of fun. Prince Kevin's big year of fun. King Kevin's lifetime of fun.

"Here Wendy," Kevin handed the card toward his drooling sister, sitting hungrily in her highchair, "Kev's got something for you."

One Last Sliver

"Startled you, didn't I? Wish you could have seen yourself in the mirror, John, when I walked into the kitchen and caught you stuffing your face full of pancakes. Blueberry, weren't they? Looked good. Made me wish I could keep the food down.

"What's that?

"Of course it's cold down here, John, it's the wine cellar. I brought you down here for a reason, so best just sit still. There are a few things I'm going to get off my chest. You keep on drinking from that bottle of Chablis. It's a fine wine, John. I know it's early but you'll grant a dying man his last wish, won't you?

"Huh?

"No, John, I don't know when they'll be back. Probably an hour, hour and a half. I gave Marie a peck on the cheek and told her I'd be fine. Lord knows I keep surprising those doctors. I told Marie it would do her a world of good to get away for even so short a while. I told her not to worry as you, John, would be here to check in on me. I told her that today was a good day. Just like that one particularly good day I had way back in 1958 when I first met Marie. It's my most cherished memory, John.

"I had just been out of the army a week when my family dragged me to an ice-cream social at church. I didn't really want to go, but it was a hot, lazy Sunday afternoon, John, you know the kind, perfect for ice cream. Marie floated in and captured my soul in that wide, playful grin of hers. She was one sweet and glorious beauty then, John. Still is. She seemed to hover on air while daring me to come join her. I don't see Marie's smile much anymore, but sometimes, before the cancer came out of remission and began to metastasize, she'd beam one my way on a quiet night as we'd sit on the deck swing, look up at the stars, and hold hands. I don't know how many times a fellow can fall in love with the same woman in one lifetime. This damned cancer's going to cut my streak short. But Marie took me in with her eyes that long ago afternoon, John, and I never cared to leave. I knew right then and there that Marie was the one I would marry and spend the rest of my life with...And I have.

"Marie's parents took me into the family fold, gave me warmth and love. It was a comfortable sweetness, John. I tried to do the same with you. God knows I tried. You'll have to excuse me if I get a little teary-eyed here, John, I miss those people...those times. Just let me wipe them off with my sleeve. There.

"You should have seen Marie on our wedding day, John, the old pictures don't do her justice. In her mother's wedding dress, my sweet Marie looked like she was up there dancing on a cloud. What a sight to behold. We were young, broke as hell, tight belts and all, but struggling, laughing and loving together. What a time that was. What a time.

"After finishing my studies at the University, John, I went to work at New Tech. I put in the long hours needed to get ahead, and eventually made it into management. New Tech was growing and I with it. I spent my entire career there. That doesn't happen much anymore these days, but you know that all too well, don't you, John?

"Time flies and goes unappreciated. Maybe I lost sight of the ball somewhere along the way, but I wanted to be a good provider for my family. I took everything seriously and, in retrospect, John, maybe too seriously.

"Did you know that Marie had two miscarriages before we had Carly? Can you imagine how that felt, John? We were so worried that we wouldn't be able to have children of our own. All through Marie's pregnancy with Carly, we prayed every day. When Carly was born, we knew our prayers had been answered. That cherub faced darling was our little miracle, John. And in the next few years we were blessed twice more. I remember like it was yesterday. Where do the years go, John? Where do they all go so quickly?

"I remember arriving home many a late night, after flying back from business trips, too many business trips, only to find little Carly sound asleep. I'd always peek in and, gently, so as not to wake her, whisper 'You're my little bunny-boo, my ittle, bittle I love you.' It may have been the moonlight shining in through the window and playing tricks, John, but I'd swear that, even in her deepest slumber, my little girl would give me a smile.

"What's that?

"Oh. Don't interrupt me, John, not during this part. I don't care if you have to go to the bathroom. Go in your pants if you must, but keep drinking that Chablis. I need to say these things as much as you need to hear them. And you are going to hear them, John.

"Did Carly ever tell you about that accident she had at Gumsrud Park? We had a picnic there when she was five. Carly slid her hand down a rickety, dried-out teeter-totter and picked up about a hundred slivers. Just imagine this little girl looking at the palm of her hand, then running to daddy. I hustled Carly home and worked on her hand with a needle for about three hours until I took every last one out. The poor little thing cried the whole time, but trusted old daddy to take care of everything. When I finished, John, Carly gave me a hug and told me she loved me. Never in my life have I felt

34

more important. I went back to Gumsrud that evening and took a sander to all the teeter-totter seats.

"I remember how, as a child, Carly used to bring home hurt animals, stray cats, dogs, you name it. Marie and I thought it such a sweet little caring. I never thought that such a sweet little caring would lead you to our door, John. Do you remember when Carly first brought you here? I sure do. I was watching from the picture window in the master bedroom, John. I watched you get out of your car, stand up, and take in my home. Your eyes swept slowly from left to right, then back again. I could practically see the engine turning over in your mind. That was when you decided to ask Carly, my little baby girl, to marry you, wasn't it?

"Huh? What's that, John?

"No, it's not my cancer talking. Of course I know how old Carly is. It's just that I'll always think of Carly as my little girl, no matter how much poison you've pumped into her mind. For sure I made mistakes. Several. The long hours and work load made me an ornery cuss at times. I've said some things that I'll always regret, and would do anything to take them back. Anything. But, goddammit John, I never deserved you...No family deserves you.

"I think one of the reasons Carly fell for you is that you were an amateur pilot. You even took her flying a few times. That's pretty exciting stuff for a young woman. You even tried to get me to buy you a cargo plane and set you up in an airline business. You wanted it all unearned and easy.

"And after I very politely declined your offer, you and Carly cut us out of your life for six months. You unlisted your phone number, no visits, no words, nothing. I believe that just might have been the year when Marie's toothy grins began to wane.

"Do you remember, John, how we paid for your trade school? And, against my better judgment, I went out on the limb and got you a position at New Tech, and when your job wasn't as cushy as you wanted it to be, you came to me with all your petty grievances. There was nothing I could do. I told you as much. I had pulled all the nepotism strings I knew just to get you that position, yet you still weren't happy. You wanted more from me, John, always, always more. I don't think you've ever stuck with a job longer than two years? And your tune was always the same. Those ignorant boss bastards had it in for you, didn't they, John?

"You parlayed my strictness, my tough love, my idiosyncrasies, and all my bad moments into a civil war. You worked on Carly in order to turn my warts into a blood feud. Do you ever realize how co-dependent Carly has become on you, John, in a sickish manner that, in her mind, substitutes for love? The poor girl can't recognize that sweet little caring anymore.

35

"You made Carly confront us with every wrinkle from the past in order to bleed us dry. Evidently, the only way we could make it up was to give you money, John. And we did, and we did, and we did. We made the down payment on your house. We bought you a car. For crying out loud, John, we helped furnish your house. What more did you want from us?

"But we loved it when Haley was born. That beautiful little peach used to follow her grandpa everywhere. In a veil of secrecy you sold your house, sold that fishing boat I loaned you, sold all your furniture, quit New Tech with no notice, and moved across country to god knows where, taking little Haley and breaking our hearts...You enjoyed bleeding us, didn't you, John?

"Don't you move, John, or I'll end what I have to say real quick. And you will not be happy with the outcome. But you've never been a happy man, have you? Even if I'd done A, B or C differently, you'd still spite me forever and all because of that vindictive bucket of piss and vinegar you've carried along your whole life.

"Do you know how many nights I held Marie while she cried and prayed for Carly and Haley's safe return? Eight years, John. Eight long years. You aged us. Do you know how you stole a piece of my sweet Marie's life? I think you do. You took great delight in using little Haley as a pawn against us. You used her to gut us emotionally. Then, after eight years of nothing, of not knowing whether you're alive or dead, of not seeing our granddaughter, of being worried sick, you show up after word gets to you that I have cancer and won't make the New Year.

"But now it's death bed conversion time. Worm your way back into the trust funds and will, right, John? You know something, John, you didn't have to show up this last month for this embarrassing, fraudulent display of regret and affection. We never took Carly out of our will. You would still have gotten your money, not enough for you, though. There's never been enough for a guy like you, John, huh-uh. Everybody is against you. Your whole life has been so tough, what with Carly working to support you all these past years. Let's everybody pity poor, martyred John. I can just picture, in my mind's eye, exactly how you'll prey on my sweet Marie as soon as I'm gone. Will your badgering of her start at my wake, John, or perhaps the next day?

"I see you've finished that bottle of Chablis. Didn't take that long, did it? Kind of reminds me of the olden days. Did I miss any new adventures at the detox these past eight years, John? Oh wait, I do apologize, I hear you've been dry since Carly threatened divorce last summer.

"Huh?

36

"Oh, you know how it goes, word from Carly's old friends kind of filters in, John, makes my ears perk up. Threat of the old meal ticket taking a hike making you clean up the old act, huh?

"Well now, I'm not a betting man, but I'd lay even money that there was something a little more than your drinking that was involved, wasn't there, John? Something Carly would be too ashamed to tell old dad or ever share with her friends. I have this strong hunch that at the end of a long, hot day, after downing a few cold ones, there might have been a little slappy-slap here, maybe a little chokey there, just to let the pissant in-laws, the shitheel bosses, and all the other faceless bastards know that, by god, John is still very much in control of his universe.

"...Did you do that to my little girl, John?

"Don't avert your eyes from me, that's more telling than not. It may sound totally crazy to you, and maybe it is, but this final stage of cancer, my being this close to death, has somehow managed to give me a third eye, John. And things have never been so clear. So you damn sure don't want to lie to me. Not now. Not here.

"What?

"Of course you've changed, John, of course. Turned over a new leaf, haven't you? And we both know it would never happen again, don't we? Stuff like that never does.

"It really would have been best for all concerned, John, had you just stayed away. But no, the hungry slot machine that is your conscience brought your poison back to my door. I loathe you for coming back to disquiet my final days, John, for making me loathe you now, just when I needed a softer landing. But mostly, I loathe you for what you did to my sweet Marie's heart and what you've made of my little Carly.

"Late last night, as I lay shivering in bed, where I've been for the past two weeks since the hospital sent me home to die, I could feel it. My god. What was happening to me? It was such a sweet, glorious feeling after all the pain of the last year. This feeling made me think of Marie and of a 1958 ice-cream social I once attended. What on earth was happening to me? I almost surrendered to this sweet, glorious feeling. But something made me resist with the little might I had left. You see, John, there was this one last thing I needed to do for my family...for my sweet, wonderful Marie and for my darling daughter. There's just this one last sliver I need to remove from my little girl's finger. For all my faults, John, which you have rubbed in my nose on endless occasions, I have always been a good provider. And today, John, has been a very good day.

"You were so depressed over my condition, over your treatment of my family, over all of your numerous failures, John, that you just couldn't bear to go on. Your playing of the grieving, remorseful son-in-law has been witnessed by all. And, of course, you began to drink again. Good lord, look at that empty bottle of Chablis – and it's not even noon. Why, John, you must have been intoxicated. You knew about the gun cabinet – where this revolver was kept – and you obviously discovered where the keys were hidden.

"...Who would ever have imagined that you'd go before me, John?

"After taking care of some rather minor logistics, perhaps a quick call to the authorities about a loud noise I heard from downstairs, I'll crawl back into bed, the same bed I've shared with Marie throughout these many, many years, and I'll wait for that sweet, glorious feeling to return, to go back to my ice-cream social, again, for a longer stay. And you know something, John? I have an inkling that I won't have long to wait.

Tongue Lashings

In retrospect, the news stories suggested, we should have seen it coming.

But those of us that lived around the Applegates; upstairs, downstairs, down the hall; took turns calling the police whenever his screaming got too loud. What more can you expect neighbors to do? Unfortunately, community housing does not a full community make.

Sure, you're kind of aware of each other in the broadest sense of the word. That drop-dead blond who leaves for work about the same time as you. That lonely, old guy who sits in the lobby watching for the mailman every Saturday afternoon. The smokers, out having a puff on the decks lining the parking lot, always give you a friendly nod as you walk past. The odd assortment of characters you bump into in the laundry room. And, of course, Margaret in the Pallisades Rental Office, who seems pleasant enough as long as your rent comes in on time.

The Pallisades is ten separate complexes of apartment buildings, a couple pools and tennis courts, as well as an underground garage for those willing to cough up a little extra. My pre-Pallisades life? After having gone cheap on rent in the few years since college, I found it hard to get some good Zs when the neighbors looked like extras from a Charles Bronson movie. Figuring that the price tag at the Pallisades would keep some of the seedier elements out, I'd moved in almost a year ago. Eden. Tahiti. Valhalla in suburbia. The Pallisades were smooth, silken, peaceful—that is, until the Applegates arrived.

The unit above me had been vacant for months. I was at work the day they moved in. Didn't notice a thing. I wasn't aware of their presence until Mr. Applegate's first major soliloquy, some night's later, ripped me awake. Disoriented, I stared at the clock. It was around midnight. I'd been asleep a couple hours. I put my head back down on the pillow when I heard the Kong-like roar. My head snapped back up. I'd never heard anything from the previous tenants. I couldn't make out what Mr. Applegate was saying, but the muffled rage and guttural sound raised the hair on the back of my neck. The man went on for a few minutes in this manner, then ceased. I figured maybe he'd stubbed his toe or something, then let loose with a few choice words.

In the beginning, the rantings didn't seem to last as long. Or perhaps it took longer to wake me, so I may have missed both the overture and portions of Act I. I'm a guy who needs eight hours of sleep a night or I'm shot the next day – all jetlagged out. It's kind of a biorhythm thing, sleep patterns and all that. I hear some people need only five or six hours. I have no idea how they get by.

Applegate's harangues seemed purposeful. Eventually it occurred to me that the shouting episodes were directed at Applegate's woman. He screamed at his wife, according to the names listed on the row of mailboxes in the main entryway. So, over the course of the next couple weeks, I assumed that the Applegates had some issues to work out. Moving can be, after all, fairly stressful. But by the end of the month I'd come to the single conclusion that Mr. Applegate was stark, raving mad.

I wish I could say that I didn't just lie there, shivering gutless in bed, eyes wide, trying to hear what all the verbal thunder was about. I lacked the prerequisite courage to bang on the ceiling as, with the earth-quaking fury inherent in his tirade-du-jour, I knew Mr. Applegate was out of control and figured he'd come down, kick the door in, and squeeze on my throat.

I first met Mrs. Applegate in the laundry room. She may have been 5'1" if she didn't look all fetal positioned up. I smiled, mumbled "Hi," and received a quick head dart and sideways nod in return. I could tell that eye contact didn't exist in her world. Carrying my clean clothes back to my room, I nicknamed her Mousey. It seemed somewhat apropos.

Mount Saint Helens didn't quit for six days. Applegate didn't quit. Period. His tongue-lashings of Mousey had to be enriched by alcohol. He seemed to flare up around midnight or so. I pictured him drinking a pitcher of cheap wine to Leno, passing out for a bit, waking up, then having an epiphany regarding exactly what type of *Goddamned Bullshit* it was this time that Mousey'd put him through on that particular day. There was never a peep out of her in return. Can't imagine her ever raising her voice. Yet Mr. Applegate mined the earth's core with his baritone of angst. And just when you thought it wouldn't be physically possible to attain a further, crazed level of bile, he'd roar into an ever-loudening crescendo of muffled profanity, attain that K2 peak, then hurtle beyond. Mr. Applegate was the Pavarotti of spousal abusers.

I could hear bits and pieces, nothing enough to fill in many juicy specifics, but there seemed to be a reoccurring motif to his diatribes, a theme, a recitative of *Your Goddamned Mother*. Mousey's mother must not like Applegate, and he, by god, hated her beyond all human understanding, with a hate that was more than a hate. Mousey had looked to be in her forties, perhaps a beaten up mid-thirties. I couldn't imagine what her mom, likely retirement age and slurping senior coffees at Perkin's, could ever have done to invoke such ire in Mr. Applegate. Except, perhaps, he sensed her disapproval.

The next week, from what I could make out, was the *Amtrak Gutting* oratory. Evidently, Mousey, on Mr. Applegate's behest, had gotten tickets through Amtrak in order to save money on airline tickets. The savings turned out to be marginal. She must have put it on his credit card and, by the time he found out how much the train tickets were going to cost, it was too late to cancel.

His mad dog fury over this one had me on edge. He was so lathered up. I waited, taut as piano wire, for what had to be the eventual throttling. At least this, no doubt charming vacation, allowed for them to be gone a week, but on the night of their return, he woke me up screaming, enraged again about her *Guttin'* him *Up the Ass with Amtrak*, and all sorts of venomous *Brain-Dead! Retard! You Gotta Learn! Oh By God—You're Gonna Learn!!!* psychobabble.

Applegate's *Breadwinner* indignation's were Wagnerian. These, I found, more often than not segued into some career issues of which he had great concern. Evidently, Applegate's boss would periodically assign him some undesirable task in what must have been some conspired effort to *Screw* him *Over*. And even though he did these less-than-pleasant chores, and even though he tackled them with Aristotelian logic and Herculean resolve, Mr. Applegate demanded that Mousey comprehend that, in no uncertain terms, he was *No One's Fuck Boy, NO ONE'S!!!*

When I first saw him, I was shocked. From the rants, I'd been expecting some rabid Paul Bunyan, all set to neuter Babe with his mighty ax. Coming home from work one evening, I walked behind him coming in. I pretended to be going past the second floor long enough to see him work the lock on the apartment above mine. Geez, the guy was inches shorter than my string bean 5'11". He had an average build, reddish hair, parted on the side, and a reddish, graying beard. Applegate sported a cheap suit jacket and tie that made him anything between a never-tenured university professor or an assistant manager at Sears.

Two clues told me that this was the bully who did all the nightly barking. One was when he flicked a quick look my way. Our eyes locked momentarily and, before I awkwardly looked away, I sensed a piercing bitterness about his brow. The second was the bottle of something tucked under his arm in one of those brown bags.

Into the Applegate's second month at the Pallisades, the police began to make housecalls. I lay, head beneath my pillow, listening to the tenth reprise of his *Saddled with the Retard* monologue. Growing louder by the syllable, Mr. Applegate was boiling point red hot, when suddenly it ceased, followed by a *thump-thump-thump* to his door. I crept over to mine, looked through the peephole, then stuck my head out in the hallway to listen. It was 1:30 in the morning and the cops were up there talking to them. I heard whispered voices for about five minutes, and then the police left. Some other neighbor had finally had it with Mr. Applegate. Excellent. I realized that was what I'd been waiting for, someone else to prime the calling-the-police pump. What a glorious two weeks that bought us. Those mornings I woke refreshed and ready for work.

But by August, it began again. Like clockwork, the surrounding neighbors round-robined the police calls. I even got up the nerve to make the awkward call on two occasions. This teamwork hobbled through August, with Applegate's blood curdling howls down to once, maybe twice a week. I could sense how Applegate was working hard, concentrating deeply, in order to keep his seething under the radar until, inevitably, all gaskets blew out and Mousey needed to hear. No, it was goddamned required that she heard how he could *Get Any Piece-a-Tit* he wanted and how he was *Retard Saddled* when he should be out *Gettin' Any Piece-a-Tit* he wanted.

In early September I talked to Margaret in the Rental Office. I didn't have to say much as most of the more-vocal neighbors had already filled her in. Margaret informed me that she was aware of the issue, and had had a couple conversations with Mousey during the day. Mousey told Margaret it was the TV that was so loud, and that she was very sorry and would try to make sure that they kept it down. Margaret knew that was utter baloney and explained that she had started the documentation process, but permissive rental laws being what they were, it took an eternity to get rid of some bad apples. Poor Mrs. Applegate, Margaret ventured, was in deep denial and won't leave him or press charges. And without that, she informed me, the police could only threaten to give them a ticket if they had to come back twice in one night.

The final time that the police stopped by was about two in the morning when Mr. Applegate was getting a head full of steam going over some dinner Mousey had made for him hours earlier and how the *Cremated Steak* was like *Eatin' Indian Moccasins*. And how as *Breadwinner!*, he worked *Fuck Hard* all day and deserved eating something better *Than Some Shit-Ass Indian Moccasin*. Mr. Applegate's voice ascended like a Pacific tsunami, in wave after wave of animal fury. A force of nature. He was even able to perform a hat trick and tie Mousey's *Goddamned Mother* into teaching her how to both *Scorch Food* and *Hump Like a Dead Corpse*. Any irony in that last statement failed to register with Mr. Applegate as he howled it repeatedly, right up to the moment the police arrived.

42

The next evening, when I got home from work, squad cars filled the parking lot. A policeman wouldn't let me in the door, but Margaret appeared from out of a police car to let the man know that I lived on the first floor. Distressed, eyes red with tears, she informed me that Mousey had been killed, murdered by her bastard husband. Margaret told me how she'd spent the last hour telling police investigator's about Mr. Applegate's constant threats, and to check the call logs, she pleaded with them, check the call logs, because Mousey's bastard husband had finally killed her.

By the end of the week, they'd arrested Mr. Applegate for the murder of his wife. Several of the neighbors, myself included, gave statements regarding the numerous incidents we'd observed. One next-door neighbor had taped a few of Applegate's tirades in order to help Margaret's case for evicting them. Police logs told the story of 18 calls to this address in the relatively short time the Applegate's lived at the Pallisades. Additionally, there were numerous calls at their previous residence.

Some crime scene information came out in the newspapers and on the local news. How Mousey had been stabbed 26 times with a steak knife. How she'd been wrapped in a bedspread and stuffed halfway in the front closet. How Mr. Applegate professed to come home to find their TV, VCR, a couple of radios and other trinkets stacked by the door.

Mousey's mother testified at the trial that, sadly, Mousey's father had been abusive and, how after years of abuse, she'd finally been able to get the grit to divorce the SOB, and had tried everything in her power to persuade her daughter to follow in her footsteps. Margaret testified about how they were making a case for eviction. The neighbor next door, with the tape recordings, walked the court methodically through several of Applegate's overheated and highly irrational tantrums.

The jury shrugged off Mr. Applegate's defense that someone had broken in, and been in the process of burgling them when Mousey interrupted. Desperate, probably high on something, the perpetrator had grabbed the dirty steak knife from out of the sink and stabbed Mrs. Applegate to death. The prosecutor made mincemeat of this defense. Sure, the perp wanted to fence a clunky 15-year old television and a couple of cheap radios to get, what, maybe 10 bucks to support his crack habit. And Mrs. Applegate interrupted him, thus making the perp stab her a double dozen times because he really wanted them transistor radios. Then the perp wraps her in a bedspread and stuffs her in her own front closet, then, after that aerobic workout, drops everything, flimsy loot included, and flees the premises leaving no prints or witnesses.

Perhaps, the prosecutor suggested, the ongoing domestic abuse had, as it always seems to do, finally taken a violent turn. The multiple stab wounds, almost chopping out Mousey's liver and most of the rest of her tiny innards, screamed out as a crime of passion. Panic took over, the prosecutor furthered, and Mr. Applegate wrapped her in the bedspread, only to realize how impossible it would be to get her out of the Pallisades undetected, so he went in to work to mock an alibi, came home, doctored up some half-baked burglary scenario, and called the police. But Applegate's alibi held no water as the coroner had Mrs. Applegate's time of death clocked at early that morning.

It was a slam-dunk for the jury. Mr. Applegate got life.

Perhaps the papers were right. Perhaps someone along the line should have seen it coming. Perhaps, then, something could have been done. Poor lost Mousey. She never had a chance. Not even from the very get-go. Walked down the aisle by one monster to be handed off to another. Friendless, all self-esteem ripped out at the root, she'd accepted her particular life term without so much as a whimper. It had to be a lonely, frightened existence.

I'll always remember Mousey…

Especially that last morning, after he'd left, as I stood in the hallway and mumbled something about locking myself out, and if she'd be so kind as to let me in to use her phone. Timid, even hesitant at first, but then I suspect she remembered the pleasant face from the laundry room. Mrs. Applegate led me straight to the phone, right through the kitchen where last night's dirty dishes were stacked neatly in the sink…

I don't think there's much more for me to say. It's kind of a biorhythm thing. If I don't get my eight hours…who knows what I'll do.

The Tenth One

It was like shoveling snow on a cold winter morning. The kind of heavy, wet snow that would find dad winking at me and saying, "Hey Little Fella, how 'bout helping the old man clear some of this white stuff out of our driveway."

I guess I'm kind of small to heave-ho a shovel-full over the blowing drifts. Instead, I would push the snow into freezing mounds. Dad would come by after finishing his big, grownup size section and hoist the frosty lumps I had gathered over the edge of the hard packed snow. On those days dad would eventually look over, often not long after we'd begun, and tell me, "Why don't you go inside, Little Fella, and get mom started on the hot cocoa."

But I'd stay outside. I'd keep on shoveling in order to help him. Dad's my best friend. I'd push the heavy, white stuff until I got a headache. The back of my eyes would grow cold and numb. It was as though an icy thumbprint, like the kind we make with finger-paints, would dance in the middle of my forehead, keeping perfect rhythm with my heartbeat.

That was exactly how it felt when I first played with time. It happened on my birthday last winter. Dad and mom were going to take me to a new Disney movie that all my friends at kindergarten had seen. Then we'd come home and I'd open all my presents. And after dinner mom would slice up my chocolate birthday cake as soon as I blew out the candles. All six of them.

I got up early that Saturday. I try to keep quiet on weekend mornings, but after watching a few cartoon shows, I went back upstairs and made sure everyone was awake. I couldn't wait to get the show on the road, as dad would usually say. Mom made me blueberry pancakes, my favorite, for a late morning brunch that would see us through until we got movie popcorn. Movie popcorn is the best popcorn in the whole world. The only trouble was that the Disney movie started in the early afternoon. And, even though I can sort of tell time all by myself, mom pointed at the hands of the clock in the kitchen in order to show me where it was right now, and then to where it had to be before we would leave. In other words...Two hours. Two long hours.

I studied that old kitchen clock harder than I'd studied my wrapped presents all week long. I stared at that old black minute hand and watched it move ever so slightly each time the second hand swept by. Much too slow. I sure didn't like that minute hand. This morning was going to take forever.

Then I stared at the hour hand. The hour hand was the big, playground bully in all of this, taking great delight in keeping me away from that Disney movie. I looked at that short, little hour hand until the back of my eyes became cold. I stared at that hour hand as hard as I could. Until I felt its rhythm, its certain energy, its something elseness that I could tell was there, until the familiar spot in the middle of my forehead began to beat right in tune with that second hand. I could almost breathe the cold winter air and feel the full weight of the shovel as I tried to throw some snow over the tall drift of the...

The hour hand jerked forward a sudden, awkward notch. I felt the give. My body became tense with anticipation and I pushed as hard as I could. The hour hand began to move faster than the minute hand. I pushed until it came to the exact spot that mom had pointed out earlier.

"Grab your jacket Little Fella," Dad called from the doorway, keys in hand. "You don't want to be late for your own birthday party, do you?"

After gulping down my large pop before the Disney stuff began, I fell fast asleep against dad's arm and slept through the entire movie.

I never told my parents. I was too afraid. Maybe there was there something wrong with me? The way it made me feel so tired, maybe I was sick. Maybe I was going to get that horrible coughing thing grandma got before mom told me she'd gone to live up in Heaven. And I didn't want to go live up in Heaven. Not yet anyway. I wanted to live up in the tree house that I was helping dad build in the backyard.

I also knew that the only other occasion in which I pushed time forward would make them angry. Very angry. You see, I pushed time forward in a place that's pretty darned important to them...Church.

Pastor Pat is a great guy, but boy his sermons can sure get "long in the tooth" as dad sometimes put it. Pastor Pat always kept going on about how today's problems would be solved if we looked toward the scriptures. I looked about the church and saw how he had all the grownups' full attention. Pastor Pat was saying how the current world crisis could be easily fixed if our leaders would only look toward the Good Book instead of...

And on and on he prattled about non-tree house stuff in this low voice that made me want to make faces at the noisy toddler in the pew behind us. That was when I decided to play. Just give it a few minutes of push this time.

I squinted at Pastor Pat with all my might. I felt the cold well up behind my eyes and the pounding slowly began in the center of my forehead.

I continued to push. Right when I thought I'd pop, the congregation began walking out, exiting from the pews and down the aisle. What had happened to the offerings? The blessing? The songs?

They had already occurred. I'd given the Church service a little push. I'm pretty sure that when I push, life floods on about me. It's like that magic show dad took me to where the magician would shuffle a deck of cards, yet the Ace of Hearts kept landing on top. By pushing time I seem to be able to reshuffle the boring hours downward into the bottom of the deck. I wanted to share my secret with dad, but I knew he and mom would see red. They would probably make me go apologize to Pastor Pat and he can be pretty stern at times.

I only pushed time backwards once. That's how I know that used-up time is almost impossible to budge. There's a small bit of give at the beginning, but then you hit a brick wall. It becomes too darned solid. Cast iron. Like mother's pancake griddle. I remember when one of my baby teeth fell out and I explored the gap with my tongue. There was a little push, but only a little wiggle room until my tongue pressed hard against the new tooth that was coming in.

I was running one of my Hot Wheels on the kitchen table when dad asked me to help him rake the yard. I kept telling him no. I told him that I wanted to play with my Hot Wheels and that he could rake the crummy leaves all by himself.

"I'm afraid I'm not asking you anymore, Little Fella," Dad said in a voice signaling his seriousness. "I would like to have your help raking the leaves. I don't think that's too much for me to ask."

"You go out and do it yourself," I cried. "You're not my best friend anymore. You go away right now. I don't like you."

Dad stood there silently, stared at me, then looked down at his feet. I'd hurt daddy by saying such mean things. He's my best friend in the whole world. And I hurt him. I hurt daddy. I'd have done anything then to take it back. And I did. The tears welled up in my eyes as I caught time.

It surprised me. Pushing backwards was so much harder than the shoveling push. It was as hard as when I was at the park where dad taught me how to do pull-ups on the monkey bars. I'd try to do ten but I could never make it past nine, and there I'd hang, kicking my feet at the empty air below me as if that would somehow magically lift my chin up and over that darned metal bar. I'd hang there with my neck tight and flailing legs for a whole minute or two until I'd drop into my father's powerful hands.

"That tenth one can be awfully tough on a little fella," dad would say and mess up my hair. "That tenth one can be awfully tough."

I was hanging from the monkey bars in my mind yet sitting there at the kitchen table. Dad's head came up and his mouth moved in a strange, fish-like manner as he slowly swallowed his previous sentence. That was when I ran straight into the brick wall, felt everything slip, and dropped.

"I'm afraid I'm not asking you anymore, Little—"

"Daddy, I love you." I jumped off my chair and ran to him. "I'm so sorry, Daddy. I love you."

"Jeez, Little Fella, I love you too." Dad picked me up in his comforting arms and gave me a hug. "It's just some yard work, shouldn't take too long. Hey, you're all white. Are you feeling okay?"

As soon as I helped dad with all the raking, I took an all-afternoon nap.

My father is my best friend. Even when he's upset about something. Just last week, as we were watching the evening news, he got up and turned off the TV. He looked real sad.

"Are you okay?" mother asked.

"It just doesn't sound good," dad shook his head. "Not sounding good at all."

"What's the matter, Dad?"

Mother turned her full attention toward me. "Oh Honey, It's a big argument between countries."

"Countries argue?"

"Remember how it is if you get into an argument with some other little boy in class?"

"Yeah."

"You know that what you're supposed to do is shake hands and be friends, right?"

"Yeah, that's what the teacher tells us to do."

"It's what you should do, Honey," mother nodded. "It's what we should all do."

"Hey Little Fella," dad smiled at me, "what say we go out and see how high you can go in that tire swing?"

"Sure Dad."

The alarm began screeching halfway through dinner. It continued in a shrill, unnerving pitch. Then white, blinding light from out of nowhere broke through the windows.

"No!" dad's eyes were wide as he looked from mother to me. "Oh dear God! No!"

I felt flush with heat. A stifling, prickly heat. Summer, sauna heat. I couldn't breathe. My lungs weren't working right. Windows were smashing inward. The entire house shook with a sound as though some monster locomotive was bearing down on us from the clouds. The noise thundered louder, became deafening. Piercing light scorched from everywhere. The house began to shudder in a violent wind I'd never known before. Dad stood up then, right as the roof began to peel like so much skin off an orange.

I shut my eyes right then and pulled. Let it work. Please let it work. I felt the familiar tingling. Suddenly I was on the monkey bars again. My chin was nearing the bar. And I pulled harder than I'd ever done before. My fingers gripped in tight circles as I pulled all of my weight upward. My neck stiffened as I probed deeper, pulled harder, worked that heavy snow over the tall drift. The cold thumbprint pulsated something fierce in the middle of my forehead. My feet flailed as my chin became even with the bar.

All noise abruptly vanished. The twisting wind ceased. I dared to open my eyes. The roof was frozen. Part torn off and gone. Part suspended in mid air. My mother's face was a cobweb of dusty cracks, welts and syrupy blisters. Her hair in tatters, with dried clumps of it laying on the table about her salad plate. I held on. It needed more. Just a little bit more. I pulled with both my hands, with all my strength, my legs fluttering at the air beneath my chair as I struggled to get ever upward.

It was the tenth pull-up. I could do it. I had to do it. I concentrated as mother's face slowly returned back into dad's "porcelain angel" as he would lovingly call her whenever he stole a quick kiss on the side of her cheek. The roof silently began to uncoil and settle. Out of the corner of my eye I saw my father, my best friend, slowly sit back down in his chair.

And then I hit the brick wall. The place where I could pull no further. Used time can only back up so much before it dead ends completely. But for the first time, the very first time, my chin was above the bar. If dad could only speak, I'm sure he'd be so proud of me.

I can feel all of my muscles tremble and shake as I hang here. My neck is as stiff as a tree branch. My ears feel as though they're going to explode. The pulsing thumbprint is beating wildly like a fire drum. So is my heart. I don't know how much longer I can hang on. And if anyone's going to save us, they'd better come soon...

This tenth one can be awfully tough on a little fella.

The Acceptance

J. Flesher Locke, III, sped toward his father's vacation home, a two hundred acre estate set deep in the East Hampton's seashore. At this time of night the roads were quiet, and he could let the Jaguar XKR do exactly what it was built for. Although it was autumn, the air a crisp fifty degrees Fahrenheit, he'd left the convertible down and let the fall breeze stream through his hair. Besides, how could he let the chill bother him after a triumph like today's?

He'd knocked it so far out of the ballpark that all of New York had to have heard about his home run. After today no one could ever again shout nepotism. Sliding out of Harvard and straight into his father's firm, Flesher put in the eighty-hour weeks to show all his colleagues that he wasn't just a second generation dunce cap hitting on the secretaries. Pretty hard to accuse someone of skating by when he'd successfully turned the stock on the TechNetData IPO, and walked away with two hundred and fifty very cool million. Just like his father, Flesh loved the game. Sure, he'd had sound guidance from his father and Uncle Walsh, and why not with this kind of money involved? But it was Flesher who'd done the homework, threaded the needle, kept his patience during the expected start-up phase, and, when the IPO opened at one-sixty and a quarter, even higher than Uncle Walsh had anticipated, the Street knew he'd arrived.

Against all instincts telling him to let it fly, Flesher braked the XKR at the intersection. It was good that he had stopped as a lone car emerged suddenly out of the mist. It was an old Buick, and the crossroad had the right of way. Flesher squinted his eyes against the high beams, and felt it beginning to happen. The car flew past, kicking up gravel in the same manner it had done on all previous occasions. Oh no. Not today. Of all days, please not today. In the nether light and haze, Flesher saw the figure, the small boy peeking out the back-side window, hands cupping the sides of his face. Their eyes locked for an instant of infinity, and Flesher shivered at the small boy's alarm.

He closed his eyes. Flesher had talked to no one about this reoccurring vision. What way could he tell anyone of it that wouldn't land him on some shrink's couch? It had been occurring more and more of late. In the light of day, he simply wrote it off as a neighbor heading toward town. But how could the image be the same, over and over again? A little boy peeking in fright and terror. Their eyes lock. And then it passes.

Flesher yanked the wheel to the right, and began following the car, the first time he'd done this. He made out the Buick in the fog, its taillights pulling ahead. Flesher pushed the accelerator, seventy-eighty-ninety, to the point of danger, yet the Buick was gaining distance. This can't be happening. No matter how souped up the Buick is, it cannot possibly outrun a Jaguar XKR. Not out in the open like this. Not on these roads. Seconds later the taillights disappear in the dust. The car was gone.

But Flesher knows the phantom Buick will be back.

My father and Uncle Walsh were seated around the mahogany desk in dad's corner office of the Manhattan tower named for my grandfather. Seventy flights up provides a spectacular view of the city. I stand in the hallway, my back toward the special facility that allows dad to turn his office into a war room—a place where he can live around the clock whenever a major acquisition takes place. Behind me is a full suite that the Four Seasons would be proud to own. Since mother's death, dad had taken to living here more and more.

Uncle Walsh isn't really a blood relative. I've called him "Uncle" my whole life. He's been Dad's right-hand man, number-cruncher savant with an uncanny nose for money and opportunity, for as far back as I can remember. They are toasting the TechNetData deal. I try not to show my giddiness, but it bleeds through every pore. It may not be the money, although that certainly greases the wheels. A father looking at his son with deep heartfelt pride, grabbing his shoulder, smiling widely, and exclaiming "That's my boy!" is what truly makes me tick.

"You know," father looks at Uncle Walsh, sips some more champagne, and nods in my direction, "this was the kind of deal I always thought he'd cut his eye teeth on."

"Ah yes." Uncle Walsh looks over my head and smiles. He gets up, walks around the desk, and pats my father on the arm. "We made a little history this past week. You got dinner plans, Jim? Let me take you to Maury's."

"Thanks, Ted, but I think I'll just plod around here tonight. It's been a roller-coaster of a month. I find that I'm very tired."

Uncle Walsh stands by father for several seconds. "If you need me, Jim, give me a call. A victory like TechNetData deserves celebrating."

Uncle Walsh leaves. Dad finishes his drink, stares toward me for a long time, then looks up. His shoulders begin to quiver. A lone tear works its way down from the corner of his eye.

"Father, are you okay?"

Dad says nothing. He continues to stare over my head. Then he put his head down into both shaking hands. I hear him sob.

"Father?" My feet are glued to the floor. "Father?"

My words appear to fall on deaf ears. I turn around and stare up at the framed picture over the doorway, the picture my father seemed focused on. Dad seems a hundred years younger. No gray hair. I look at the other figure in the picture with him. My heart catches deep in my throat. The little boy looks so happy to be in this picture with his father. The little boy who lived for the twinkle in his father's eye. The same little boy I've seen repeatedly in the back of that Buick on misty, fog-filled nights.

With a desolate clarity I realize that the little boy is not an apparition...

It's night. I'm in the Jaguar XKR. The Jaguar XKR I received as a present from dad when I graduated from Harvard. At least that's what I believe. Memories of Harvard feel skin deep, with half-remembered roommates, forgotten dates, and class projects which vaguely echo in the dark. The convertible is down, but I feel no chill. I don't recall ever feeling a chill.

Yet memories of my mother are vivid. I remember holding her hand, her smiles as she went through the chemotherapy treatment. I have a solid memory of my father walking me out of her hospital room that very last time, giving me a deep hug, and saying that he'd always be there for me. I remember the picture taken with dad, how he got me into that itchy suit, and made me giggle at the photographer's studio.

Like a writer's first draft, my later memories lack substance and touch. Who am I? Perhaps better yet, what am I? Though I don't remember braking, the Jaguar is at the intersection, stopped, as if waiting for something I know will come. Have always known will come. Out of the mist I see the Buick. My eyes, this time, wide open to the high-beams as they pass. I lock eyes with the boy, the boy who might one day have grown into me. And now I'm certain. The little boy is not the apparition...I am.

In a kaleidoscope of colors, the Jaguar XKR dissolves. It was never real. Rather a focal point, a bridge for my acceptance. And as I accept, a floating sensation overtakes me. The Buick's taillights are suddenly far below me, and, swirling though mist and devoid of time, I follow.

The little boy is scared. A man pulls him from his bed. He is carried down to a running car. He sees the housekeeper on the floor, a pool of blood pillowing below her head. The man carrying the boy smells of B.O. and ashtrays. The boy is shoved into the back seat of a car. A bigger man jumps behind the steering wheel, stares at the boy, stares down with furrowed pig's eyes that dart back and forth, running over him like a Xerox machine. The ashtray man sits next to him as they speed from the driveway. Miles away, he sees lonely headlights at a stop sign. He cups his eyes and stares out into the darkness. His eyes lock briefly with those of a young man driving a convertible. What feels like electricity passes through him. When he turns to see if the young man is following, he sees nothing.

They're in a dilapidated farmhouse. He's locked in a corner room, with sheets of plywood nailed over the window. Torn blankets are his bed. The man who smells of ashtrays gives him baloney, stale crackers, and luke-warm water a couple of times a day. Pig Eyes walks him to the filthy restroom whenever he has to go. The little boy misses his father. The father who swore he'd always be there for him. He thinks these men want money. He wonders if Clora, his nanny, is all right—or was she dead.

A week passes. He hears someone pull up. He hears talk in the outer room. The ashtray man lets out a string of profanity. He hears a noise as if things are being tossed off a table. Pig Eyes opens the door, grabs his arm, and drags him out into the main room. He sees his Uncle Walsh. A smile sweeps across his face. They've come for him. His father and Uncle Walsh have come for him. But something is strange. Where is daddy?

"Thanks to these numb-nuts killing the housekeeper— your father went against my better judgment, for the first time, ever, and brought in the Feds." Uncle Walsh walks over and rubs the boy's hair. "Sorry 'bout this Jimmy, m'boy." Uncle Walsh turns, tosses a thick envelope at Pig Eyes, and heads toward the door. "But sometimes you've got to eat the margins."

The little boy is marched off into the woods. Shadows of the tall trees darken the forest path. Pig Eyes grunts, tells him to stop, then pushes him to the ground. The little boy thinks of his father. More than anything else, he wants his daddy.

I am standing in the woods on the exact spot where it happened those many years ago. Where a little boy's life ended, and, in a peculiar way, mine began. So is this who I am? The what-might-have-been, beckoned by a father's never-ending love for his son. An apparition borne from the womb of a father's bottomless grief…And a little boy's cry for justice. I wish I could see my father one last time, touch his cheek, let him feel the love, and grant him the peace he so desperately needs—yet I know it can't be so.

For I have a different purpose. And at last I realize what I must do. Indeed, there shall be some last visits. One to a brutal man with the eyes of a pig, one to a bully who smells of an ashtray, and, finally, a very special visit to a betrayer I'd once referred to as "Uncle."

Flesher knew that his wasn't a violent soul...But sometimes you have to eat the margins.

Entitlement Cuts

Goddamned Styrofoam cup. Granger had set the cup, steaming with coffee, between his thighs as he made a right turn onto 3rd street. Hot sugared coffee had sloshed up through the mouth flap and splashed onto Granger's inner thighs. He choked back a profanity and steered the agency's car to the side of the road. A lady in a Ford Bronco gave him an impatient tap of her horn just as Granger edged off the blacktop and onto the gravel. What the...! Granger whipped his head sideways; shot her both a stern glare and the one finger salute as she sped by. This jerking movement caused more steamy coffee to splash up and spill out onto Granger's lap.

How much longer did he have to put up with this endless shit? Although Granger was on time for his ten o'clock appointment, he felt like bagging it and heading home. But then he would miss the incentive bonus, and he was so close to completing the next level. Granger's interim performance appraisal had been, well, satisfactory. You will never soar with the eagles if you attain a mere "meets requirements" performance rating. And that damned Renke! That goddamned Renke? Here they have Granger driving all over backass creation for out state appointments while Renke gets the posh metro accounts. And the fartskull overseers blindly wonder why Granger only "meets requirements." Renke will win the Hawaiian quota package, hands down, while Granger gets to drive through endless armpit country. Granger gets to wreck his eyesight squinting at the connect-a-dot lines on the county map that constitute the pot hole filled roads in the grim grid that represents his territory.

And now these very same government bureaucrats have lowered the quota demographics to eighty. That meant a mountain of more work stacked high atop of Granger's currently uncompleted pile. Granger's anger had grown during the quota meeting last week. He had gently informed his superiors that his plate was full, and that his current client load kept him jumping. But then Renke had interrupted, cutting him off at the knees, by telling the bean counters that he didn't foresee any difficulties in attaining the new goals set by the regional management. Granger sat and burned as the overseers smiled and patted Renke on the back. He wanted to wipe that smug look off Renke's face right then and there. Give me the metro run, Granger thought, and I'll take the Maui package every goddamned year. One of these days, in the not too distant future, a team of proctologists would have to surgically remove his size thirteen from Renke's ass.

Granger pulled into the parking lot. He glanced through the overdue O'Reilly account. Granger put on his hat and walked quickly into the complex. He didn't stop by the receptionist's station as O'Reilly's file gave Granger the correct suite number. Granger took the steps up to the third floor and stood outside room 314. He looked down the hallway in both directions. Not much activity going on today. He paused for a second and peeked into the room. An elderly man in a robe and pajamas sat on a bed propped up by numerous pillows. The television was on with the volume set annoyingly high.

"Are you O'Reilly?" Granger entered the room.

"What?" asked the elderly gentleman.

"Are you Eugene O'Reilly, born December 12th, 1909?" Granger had to shout above the roar of the TV.

"Yes, I'm Gene. Who are you?"

"Could you please turn the television down?" Granger shut the door.

"Sure will young man." O'Reilly dug about his bedspread for what seemed to Granger like an eternity. Upon finding the remote buried under one of his many pillows it took a lesser eternity for him to find the volume control and turn the television down to a whisper.

"Thank you," Granger said as he stooped by the door as if to tie his shoe. "I'm the regional account representative from the Social Security Office. You're one of my cases."

"What?" O'Reilly asked again, "Who are you?"

"I'm the regional account rep from the United States Social Security Office," Granger crossed the room and sat in the visitor's chair across from O'Reilly. "We've been wondering just how long you thought you'd be able to pull it off?"

"What?" O'Reilly sneezed into the sleeve of his robe.

"How long did you think you were going to be able to pull all this off?"

"Pull what off, Sonny?" A puzzled O'Reilly shook his head, "My social security is taken care of by Mrs. Johnson in administration. You need to see Mrs. Johnson in administration."

"You know, Eugene, I've had a bad day. I almost got lost finding my way here, and then I spilled hot coffee all over my lap. Any future kids of mine are gonna need skin grafts."

"Ouch," O'Reilly gritted his dentures.

"Look Eugene," discussions like these were not part of Granger's job, actually they went directly against agency policy, but he felt a certain bedside manner was called for, "The Wright brothers were at Kitty Hawk when you were born. You retired in 1972. You've been in this nursing home since 1988. Enough is enough, Eugene. Just how long did you think you were going to get away with it?"

"I'm not sure I know what you mean young man," O'Reilly was becoming irritable, "but I'm going to call for—"

Granger grabbed the bed frame and wheeled it, O'Reilly included, away from the assistance cord. "Frankly, Eugene, every time you fart Medicare gets a bill for five K. You had to suspect it wouldn't last forever."

"Listen," O'Reilly was now enraged, "I have no idea what you're talking about. I paid into social security. That's my money."

"You never paid into Medicare, Eugene. And your piddly contribution to Social Security dried up at the teat when peanut farmer ran the circus. Hell Eugene," Granger chuckled, "You've been living off welfare for over twenty years now. You're like one of them teenage moms."

"I want Mrs. Johnson in here immediately. She takes care of rude young men like you. I'll make sure Mrs. Johnson files a complaint with your office regarding your insolence."

"You know, Eugene, I look at my pay stubs and see how much they deduct in social security. I know full well that I'm never going to see any of it," Granger mused. "Yet my generation is forced into indentured servitude in order to support a bunch of fossils like you. Honestly, Eugene, how long did you think it'd be before we found you out?"

"But it's my money, Sonny-boy. Roosevelt made us a promise," O'Reilly protested, "Roosevelt promised."

"Well, at least FDR was thoughtful enough to check out before he turned into a blood-sucking leech on the nation's economy. Hmmm, blood-sucking leech, that sound like anyone we know, Eugene? What'd you expect, that about fifty of us would continue to whistle while we worked overtime just so you can sit here on your hemorrhoids watching 'The Price is Right' into the next millennium?"

"I've earned everything I've gotten, you rotten little bastard," O'Reilly's face had turned beet red. "I served in the military. I fought in the big war."

"I've read your silly ass file, Eugene. You were too old for combat so they put you in the mess hall. I bet they called you Cookie. You probably spent World War II drinking after-shave and screwing Filipino girls." Granger glanced down at his watch. "That was probably the best time of your life."

"That's not true!" O'Reilly wheezed and reached for his cane, "I'm going to get Mrs. Johnson and she's going to call the police. I don't know who you think you are, but I'm—"

"Oh no, Eugene, no," Granger shook his head mournfully, "I'm sorry. I know it's not your fault. It's them D.C. bastards, always raccooning into crap that'd be better off left alone. Geez, Eugene, you're one of my few lucid clients. I was hoping to sit, rest my dogs awhile, and chew the cud, but here I go again ruining it. It's pretty much the same reason the missus left me. Well," Granger walked over and took the cane out of O'Reilly's liver-stained hands, "I really must be going. Unfortunately you're not my only appointment today. I've got a one o'clock in some other Podunk down the road a stretch."

"From now on you do all your business through Mrs. Johnson." O'Reilly coughed and leaned back in his bed. "I don't care to ever see you again."

"Can't say as I blame you, Eugene. It's just crazy how much cost is involved," Granger reflected, "Absolutely mind-boggling. It finally reached the crisis point for them D.C. bastards I was telling you about. You see I'm from a sister branch of the Social Security Office, Eugene, one that never makes the headlines or TV. And I'm afraid to inform you that your account is past due. Sorry 'bout all this buddy. Time for the old glue factory."

"What?" O'Reilly caught his breath, "What do you want from me?"

"Your ghost."

"My ghost?"

Granger shrugged, "As an account rep from the United States Social Security Office, I've come to help facilitate you in the giving up of it."

"What?" O'Reilly's eyes grew wide. Realization sank in as he stared into Granger's un-budging grin.

Granger grabbed a pillow with both hands and pressed it against O'Reilly's face. Granger glanced at the door to double-check the wedge he had set in place denying access to any potential meddlers. He pressed O'Reilly down to the bed and waited. O'Reilly put up a slight struggle, but it was useless against the force of Granger's full body weight.

Granger felt the familiar stirring in the front of his trousers. And, in a moment of almost spiritual clarity, Granger realized that it was the job, the goddamned job, which kept him coming back day after miserable day. It was the rush he always felt; the pride and gratification that came from doing the job, and doing it right, that allowed him to put up with the endless driving, ridiculous work quotas, bogus incentive plans, smug co-workers, and the mediocre evaluations.

It was the job...

Cold Snap

"I'll be damned," Sheriff Holcombe hung up the phone and stared at his deputy, Jim Tate. "The medics broke off two of Moe's fingers getting him into the ambulance."

Fairmont was in the midst of a January deep-freeze, with a projected high for the day of 28 below zero. The wind-chill, currently a mean 60 below, stole your breath and freeze-dried snot to the side of your face. Exposed flesh would be frostbit in under a minute. Because of the winds, mild snowfall caused immediate drifting and blizzard-like conditions. Nights were worse. The short-term forecast was a depressing "No end in sight."

Big Moe Thorsen, proprietor of Fairmont's only strip club, D-Cups, had been missing since yesterday afternoon. Moe had been making his weekly drive home after auditing the week's take at the clubs he owned in Mankato and Lake Crystal. It was mid-morning when Sheriff Holcombe had found Big Moe's deserted Lincoln stalled out on old highway 18, just a few miles east of town. Its hood was up, warped backwards across the windshield by the wind, and with a drift of snow packed over the engine block.

Holcombe radioed both Deputy Tate and the city's only towing service. While the Lincoln was being towed back to the impound lot, both cops, shrouded in down-filled parkas, snowmobile pants, face masks and chopper mittens, took three minute turns plodding through the embankment along the side of the road. Both figured Big Moe would have headed toward town. About the time they were getting ready to send for more manpower to form a search party, Deputy Tate saw the mound, or saw a patch of black in a drift of white. It was Moe Thorsen, sporting his customary long jacket, dress Dexter's and driving gloves, all worthless under present conditions. Holcombe did his gentle best to brush away the crusty snow and ice from Thorsen's frozen body. Big Moe's face was a white welt of frostbite, his sleet-covered eyes dusty blue marbles. After the paramedics arrived, the two exhausted policemen notified the county morgue, then headed back to town for steaming hot coffee and time to thaw out.

"What the heck was he thinking?" Tate asked.

"It's dark, cold, your car dies. Not many others out on a night like this. I imagine Moe got scared. Or panicky. Don't know why he popped the hood. Maybe he thought he could jerry-rig it, get it going. His cell phone was dead. Big Moe probably hadn't recharged it for weeks, and right when he needed it most, it's fried."

"Do you suppose he thought he could walk back to town?"

"Maybe Moe assumed he could find a farmhouse or flag down a car that was either coming or going."

"Bitter winter like this sure has a humbling effect."

"Guy on the news said we're in for another week of it. Said we haven't had this fierce a cold snap since the winter of '27." The sheriff continued, "I heard down in the cities, they found a homeless guy frozen to a sewer grate. They had to dump a few gallons of boiling water over him just to get his face unstuck from the metal."

"Maybe Fairmont's getting off easy with only Moe Thorsen and that Jarvis fellow from earlier in the week."

"I should have told Jarvis's widow to have the word 'Dumbass' engraved on his headstone." Sheriff Holcombe noted the stunned expression on Deputy Tate's face and grinned. "I'm sorry. Jarvis did my tax returns. Now I gotta find a new guy before April. Jarvis was book smart, but that lush must have been down to one brain cell. I mean, unless you're drunk as hell, you don't run out to the woodpile to grab an armful of fire logs wearing nothing but tennis shoes, boxer shorts, and a T-shirt."

"Probably thought it'd only take him thirty seconds. Probably did it all the time during normal winters."

"So the wind sucks his door shut, and he's locked out of his own house. Then the dumbass, who's got six acres between his place and the nearest neighbor, fumble-farts his way around checking, I guess, to see if all the doors are locked. First thing Jarvis should've done was smash the front window with one of those fire logs."

"Must be that panicky thing. You just don't think right."

"Then he spends his last few dumbass seconds on earth thinking he's gonna triathlon it over to the neighbor's house. He only makes it to his mailbox. With his wife gone from home, no one knew until the mailman finds him all squatted over, looking like freezer-burned venison."

"One more week of this cold front is about one week too long for me." Deputy Tate stood up, "I reckon I should make the rounds. I'll cruise the highways leading in and out of town and make sure to account for the owners of any dead cars."

"Makes good sense. We don't want to send county any more Popsicles."

Sheriff Holcombe was pissed off. Major-league pissed off. After Boy Scout Tate left, it took all of the sheriff's self-control to keep from upending his oak desk. Big Moe Thorsen was about the only person for whom Holcombe would be personally out searching for; turning his gonads blue, in the middle of this cold, white hell. Moe was practically family. He and Big Moe went back almost thirty years.

It had been Holcombe who had first proposed that Moe open one of his titty bars in Fairmont, only with certain bennies that Mankato's finest would never provide. The grade A, behind-the-glass flesh was only a front. A fellow could go to D-Cups and score some dope, snort, lick, even needles, if he had the green. Big Moe had fence connections in Mankato whenever any jewelry, cameras or hot Rolexes worked their way through the club. And Holcombe got a blind eye fifty percent on every dollar. Sheriff Holcombe also personally took quick care of any competition that Big Moe had cause to complain about.

And the sheriff was still unable to fathom that Jarvis was dead. Jarvis may suck down half a bottle of Jim Beam nightly, but he was an ingenious accountant during work hours. Jarvis ran book in Fairmont—games, races, you got the coin and Jarvis was the man to see. More importantly, Jarvis set Holcombe up with a couple of lucrative, off-shore accounts to stow some of the lesser publicized perks of Holcombe's job, that is, D-Cups' kickbacks, Holcombe's share of the book, his cut (taken both under the table and in-trade) from whore mansion down on Lair Road, and, hell, more then thirty percent of the insurance dinero paid from the Thompson Trucking fire last fall. Yup, being sheriff of Fairmont County paid very well, indeed, when you tossed in Holcombe's customized portfolio and varied retirement opportunities. But, truth be known, Jarvis was the real brains behind the Grand Cayman accounts. His death was going to be a major setback.

Jarvis's wife had been staying at Gumsrud Inn, where she normally hung whenever Jarvis went on a week-long binge. If she'd been home, Jarvis would still be alive. He'd make her pay. Holcombe would make damn sure she'd be back spreading 'em at the Lair Road mansion, where Jarvis had first met her. Hell, a couple of choice words from him and Jarvis's widow will be pulling double-shifts in the Green Card room.

And what on earth was he going to do with that busybody Tate? Tate's predecessor, Deputy Cronin, had scared the bejesus out of the good citizens of Fairmont. Some of the weak-suck councilmen informed Holcombe, on the sly, that they were more than happy to see Deputy Cronin leave for his new job in the Florida Keys, even if Cronin had only given the poor sheriff one day's notice. What the councilmen didn't know about Deputy Cronin's departure last fall for some nebulous security position down in the Keys was that it had never really occurred.

Cronin and his trampy fiancée were buried under about four feet of dirt out at Stump Acres. The double-crosser had fatally underestimated the sheriff, never thinking that Holcombe would connect with Big Moe and realize that the five percent of unaccounted for snort money and Cronin's new Camaro, which had been paid for in cash, were, in fact, one and the same. Never the brightest bulb on the tree, Deputy Cronin's duplicity earned him three twenty-two slugs right in his buckteeth, compliments of Holcombe himself. As for the Camaro, it had found its way, ala Big Moe, to a chop shop in Des Moines.

After Deputy Cronin's abrupt departure, Sheriff Holcombe figured he needed a clean-cut front man for both the town folk and the city council humps. Deputy Tate seemed a dream come true, a PR poster boy with fawn-like eyes, Boy Scout manners, never a terse word, all smiles and cream. But the Boy Scout wasn't working out. Far from it. Deputy Tate was always listening, always scribbling in that notebook Holcombe could never find whenever the deputy left at the end of his shift, always asking about people and places he had no business asking about. Sheriff Holcombe needed breathing room. Especially now. His customized portfolio demanded a wide girth of breathing room.

And what in hell was all that ugly crap out at the Jarvis place? The son of a bitch Tate didn't want to leave the scene. Even after the meat wagon hauled Jarvis away, Holcombe had to order Deputy Tate to go to Gumsrud Inn and fetch Jarvis's wife. The sheriff damn near put a cap in Tate's ass right then and there. Holcombe had desperately needed some quality time to rifle through Jarvis's office for any papers that might prove a tad awkward to explain. Finding none, he had to get his ratchet wrench and go to quick work on the fireproof safe hidden behind a false wall in a basement closet. Holcombe had just gotten the damn thing plopped into his trunk when Boy Scout showed up with Jarvis's widow-whore. Tate must have done a hundred miles an hour, both ways, in order to get back so fast.

It was obvious that Deputy Tate either knew or suspected something. When he suspected trouble, Holcombe wasn't one to play child games; he was one to dig problems out at the root. Cronin and the others at Stump Acres may soon expect a new arrival. The deputy's earlier conversation with him suddenly got Sheriff Holcombe to thinking. An idea slowly began to emerge. Perhaps he wouldn't have to make the boys dig a midnight plot in this frosty, white hell.

After all, the forecast called for several more days of this winter's brutal cold front. More than enough time for there to be just one more casualty of this deep freeze...

Deputy Tate cruised the outlying highways searching for any stalled cars or stranded townsfolk in need of help. Not finding any he headed back into town. Tate saw the deserted fish shacks, empty of even the heartiest of ice-fishers, peppered across Lake Sisseton, and remembered the plywood shack he and his grandfather had nailed together and hauled out on Sisseton all those winters ago. Cruising the streets of the old downtown, the deputy noticed the Christmas lights still decorating the storefronts. Almost a month past the holidays, but still too cold for merchants to get the ladders out and remove the decorations. He passed the elementary school and noted the line of buses, idling quietly with doors shut, waiting the half hour until classes would be dismissed for the day to pick up their precious cargo. School had been canceled yesterday and one day last week, but they were going to make a go of it today so the kids wouldn't fall far behind in their studies. Tate drove slowly by, then crossed the railroad tracks and passed the graveyard where his father, both sets of grandparents, and other Tate kin lay buried.

Though the squad car was toasty, the deputy's head ached. The defrost, set on high, hummed along with his thoughts. Do the ends really justify the means? Silly question since he was way past the rationalizing stage. That particular decision had already been answered. Answered quite loud and quite clear as Tate marched an obviously blitzed Jarvis out of his own home, then stood guard in the entryway, and watched the disoriented drunkard flop around the yard, like a fish tossed ashore, as he died from exposure. Tate's decision bore compounded interest last night as he pulled Big Moe Thorsen over to the side of the road, then, at gunpoint, shoved him down into the whirling blizzard of the snow-encrusted ditch, the unforgiving wind-chill, and the darkness.

But breaking Holcombe's machine wasn't good enough. Tate was going to have to kill it. And kill it soon. Otherwise the sheriff would have it back up and running in no time. Fairmont deserved better than that. Fairmont was a good town. It was his town. Tate figured he'd stick with the same plan that had been working well so far.

All reports indicated that the arctic blast wouldn't break till week's end. Ample time, Tate reflected, for this exceptionally icy winter to take one final bite...

Sweeps Week

The fake policeman watched as the movie star drove his Porsche out through the security gate at the home of his estranged wife and sped off down the boulevard. The fake policeman left his car, walked over and slid sideways, back against the brick fence and under the surveillance camera, until he reached the car gate. He ran the magnetized card through the slot. The gate popped open. The fake policeman entered and shut the gate in one quick, fluid motion.

The fake policeman rang the front doorbell and waited. After a minute an attractive woman in her early thirties opened the door. He recognized her from recent pictures in magazines like *The Enquirer* and on shows like *Entertainment Tonight*.

"Officer," the estranged movie star's wife was surprised, "How did you get in?"

"Your husband let me in, Ma'am," the fake policeman said professionally. "I don't mean to startle you but Dr. Steicken, the plastic surgeon next door, had his house burglarized last night."

"Oh my goodness. Is everyone okay?"

"Yes. They were at a dinner party until late last night. When they got home they went straight to bed. It wasn't until this morning that they noticed several valuables missing."

"Oh no."

"We have reason to believe the burglar may have cut across part of your yard. Do you remember hearing or noticing anything unusual last night? Anything at all?"

"I didn't hear anything from outside last night, but I keep the air on and the windows closed."

"Is there anyone else here I might talk to? A housekeeper or gardener?"

"No, I'm here alone. The housekeeper only comes in for an hour or so in the afternoon."

"Ma'am, would you mind taking me through to the back yard so I can see where your property adjoins the Steicken's?"

"Sure. I feel so sorry for the Steicken's. I'll have to give them a call."

The estranged wife turned and began to lead the fake policeman toward the back of the mansion. Behind her the fake policeman quietly put on a pair of black gloves. He reached behind his belt and then began his work.

Ten minutes later the fake policeman found the PC in the upstairs office. He typed a short note. The note read simply:

Dearest Dickhead,

I have grown so very weary of your constant foot-dragging, haggling and lawyerly tricks regarding our divorce settlement. I've had enough. You *will* agree to my terms ASAP or else I go public and let your adoring, pimply fans know just how twisted a bastard you really are. And you know which stones get overturned first you impudent prick i.e. the physical abuse, the bisexuality, your happy penchant for the nose candy, et cetera, ad nauseam...
Very Truly Yours,

The fake policeman typed in the estranged wife's first name, post-dated it to the previous Monday, and stored the note into the computers' hard drive.

Upstairs the fake policeman found an enormous walk-in closet containing what had to be the movie star's clothes. The fake policeman dropped vials of cocaine into the pockets of several Armani sport jackets. In the bathroom off the master bedroom, the fake policeman dumped some of the white powder onto the vanity.

He put on a pair of loafers, an extremely tight fit, and walked downstairs through the bloody mess that had once been the living room. After a couple trips back and forth he took off the shoes and put them in a plastic bag by the entryway. Then the fake policeman went to the downstairs porch walkout and cut through one of the many screens with the bloody knife. He stacked a jewelry case, a radio, a cellular phone and the estranged wife's purse on the porch in a feeble attempt to make it appear like a burglary gone awry.

When the fake policeman put the bloody knife in the plastic bag with the shoes he heard the phone ring. He walked back to the kitchen where there was an answering machine built into the phone and waited. After the tone the caller proceeded to leave a message.

"Honey," the fake policeman recognized the entertainment world's most famous voice immediately, "Are you in the shower or something? I just wanted to remind you to make the reservations for tonight, okay. I look forward to seeing you. Love ya Hon."

The phone clicked and the fake policeman smiled. He could not have planned it any better.

The fake policeman drove past the gate of the movie star's rented mansion in Beverly Hills. He parked his car at the end of the block. The fake policeman took out one of the bloody shoes, looked both ways, stepped out of the car, and flipped the shoe into the foliage on the other side of the cement fence.

At the movie studio he was now a phony security guard. As he walked through the secured parking lot he had a handkerchief cupped in the palm of his left hand. As he passed the Porsche, the now phony security guard gently wiped the handkerchief against the passenger's door handle, the side-view mirror and the front headlight.

At lunch the phony studio security guard was able to slip into the prop room unnoticed. He had done a poor job of wiping the knife with the handkerchief. A close examination would reveal the dried blood to even the most untrained of eyes. He haphazardly dropped the knife on top of the real props in one of the numerous cabinets.

The ex-fake policeman and formerly phony security guard, having recently changed in a restroom stall, contemplated the missing links as he walked out to his car. The missing links were the icing on the cake, making it all that more delicious. This would make the O.J. trial look like a PBS documentary. With unheard of billions spinning through his mind, the representative from the Multi-Media Consortium slid behind the wheel of his car, steered toward the studio exit gate, and headed into the city.

The Inheritance

The Past

"They're in there." Grandma Barnes' fingernails dug deep into my forearm. "Your mommy and daddy don't believe me, Michael." Grandma's gray hair was in tatters, her makeup smeared by the tears, "But they're in there, all right. Waiting. Breathing. Scratching." Her trembling finger pointed toward her bedroom door, "Always scratching. Wanting to come out and—"

"Mother!" Mom rushed up the staircase. "Stop it now, Mother. You're scaring Michael. He's just a little boy."

I was five at the time. My parents and Aunt Carol had driven over to Grandma's house after meeting with her doctor, and then making preliminary arrangements at the nursing home. Something had to be done. As an only child, I fluttered with my toys in the background while half paying attention to them as they took care of this family emergency.

Grandpa Barnes had died before I was born. Grandma Barnes continued to live alone in their house. Grandma was almost seventy, and had recently become frightened and unstable. She wasn't acting at all like the grandma who used to sing old nursery rhymes while rocking me to sleep. My parents did their best to paint a cheerful picture and explain that grandma was just getting "a little different" due to her advanced age. That was over thirty years ago. Nobody knew about Alzheimer's. Back then this behavior was filed under the general category of senility. Grandma was just getting "a little different" due to the onslaught of senility.

The changes in her were first noticeable last summer when grandma began complaining to my father about the noises. About strange breathing noises which she heard mostly at night. About the strange scratching sounds, strange creaks. My dad had a repairman check her furnace and water heater. Both were in fine condition, the furnace having been replaced recently. Dad told grandma that she was just hearing the sounds of her old two-story settling.

My parents contemplated having grandma come live with us, but Aunt Carol had none of that. This house, according to my childhood eavesdropping of Carol, represented grandma and grandpa's life together. This was grandma's house and she would live there as long as she was able to. But that was before the hushed calls began coming in the middle of the night.

"They live in the closet," Grandma would urgently whisper to mother in the post midnight phone calls. "I can hear them breathing. My god, I can hear them scratching. Help me. Come help me now."

After the third or fourth time that dad rushed over at three A.M., slid open the doors of grandma's closet and showed her that no one, and no thing, was in there, Aunt Carol began to come around to my parents' point of view. They began checking into the care provided by the nursing homes in town. If Grandma Barnes was suffering from senility, she would need more help than we could ever provide at our home.

It hit a crises zone when grandma began to call the police in the dead of night to have them come over and "get the things" that were in her closet. After a couple of weeks of responding to grandma's midnight calls, the police contacted Aunt Carol and informed her as to what was occurring.

As I walked around the old two-story house hitting my whiffle ball with my plastic bat, my parents and Aunt Carol were downstairs discussing the situation with Grandma Barnes.

"I'm not crazy!" I heard grandma insist at one point. "I'm not!"

"Now mom, we're not saying that. It's only that we don't think you should be living alone here if you—"

And off I went running through Grandma Barnes' upper floor. Her two-story had been built around the turn of the century. Although it had an antiquated look, and feel, Grandma had kept her home in mint condition. There was lots of hard wood and plenty of places to hide. I'd been batting the toy ball from room to room and thinking about Grandma Barnes' frantic warning. I loved grandma and didn't really understand what she was going through. But she had stated to me that "they're in there, all right" and, in the best Tom Sawyer spirit, I slowly made my way toward the main bedroom.

I batted the whiffle ball down the hallway. The ball flew through the air with a whooshing sound. I walked past the guest bathroom to retrieve my ball. I stood down the hall from grandma's bedroom and stared at the open door.

The room beyond stood quietly, as though patiently awaiting a formal introduction. Through it I could see grandma's brass bed and beyond that her table of knickknacks. I was forbidden to play in Grandma Barnes' bedroom because of her antique collectibles. My parents felt, not without justification, that I could be the proverbial bull in the china shop.

Seconds passed while I got up the nerve. I looked back to see if anybody was coming. The coast was clear. I hit the ball through the open doorway, watched as it bounced off the wall and disappeared from sight. I walked to the doorway, stood in the frame, and turned left. Grandma's closet had giant, bifold doors. The kind of doors that when you slid the handles sideways, the hinged partitions would bend outward in a V-shape. Fan doors I think they used to call them. Grandma's bifold door partitions had the old-fashioned, downward wooden slats that could collect heavy dust if grandma let them. And from the looks of them, she'd been letting them.

As I studied grandma's closet from this sideways angle, I could see that the doors were halfway slid open. The whiffle ball, having bounced off the far wall, had rolled to a stop. It rested in front of grandma's closet. A quarter of my plastic ball was obscured by the partially opened doors. I started toward the center of grandma's bedroom when the whiffle ball disappeared.

I stopped in my tracks. The ball had come to a complete stop, momentarily sat still, then abruptly went inside. I remembered going to the Funhouse at the State Fair. Some of the floors there were slanted. You could place a bowling ball on the floor and watch it roll. But this was not the Funhouse at the State Fair. How could my ball come to a complete stop, then start again? It made no sense. Unless it got...yanked inside. As I stood confused in the center of grandma's bedroom, staring at the partially opened bifold doors and into the darkness beyond, I heard the noise.

It was a low sort of human noise, an exhaling sound that reminded me of an exhausted sprinter upon completion of a trying dash. Except that all corresponding inhaling sounds were...missing. Just a continual huh-huh-huh sound that I couldn't exactly place. The closet door was accordioned half sideways. Inside the triangular bend of the bifold doors would be a great cranny for a small child to win in a game of hide and seek. I'd even hidden in dark spaces like this before. The exhaling noise was soon followed by a light scratching noise. Very light. A razor sound. A razor on hard wood. I stared down to seek out the source.

My parents had recently taken me to a pet store. I was fascinated with the parakeets. Especially the way in which they could stand on their perch. Their claws would wrap backwards around the wooden bar on which they stood. The talon I saw reaching out from the half-inch space between the floor and the bottom of the V in grandma's bifold door reminded me of that day in the pet store. Only this claw was bigger—longer and thicker, much thicker— than that of any parakeet.

My blood curdled. The talon scratched long, figure eight's in the hard wood floor. My throat became a dry lump. I stood watching the movements in what seemed like a hypnotic trance. I couldn't move my legs. The exhaling sounds had become quicker, guttural, louder...

...And more than just one.

"Michael!" My mother yelled for me from the downstairs living room, "Michael, where are you?"

69

That broke my hesitancy. I flew from Grandma Barnes' room, down the staircase, and into the safety of my mother's embrace.

"It's in Nanna's closet," I cried, the warm tears streaming down my face. "They're in Nanna's closet."

"You see now, Mother," my mom looked toward grandma with saddened eyes. "You've scared Michael with all this foolish talk."

I tried to describe what I'd seen, or thought I'd seen, but no one, except Grandma Barnes, truly listened. And, after dad checked out grandma's closet for now the umpity-ump time and found nothing, I began to doubt myself. I hung tightly to mom but said no more. I didn't want them to think that I was getting just "a little different" and then tuck me away in a nursing home. But I never went back upstairs.

It was decided that Aunt Carol and my mother would alternate staying overnight with Grandma Barnes until the arrangements at the nursing home were finalized. They would leave the main bedroom empty. Grandma would sleep in mom and Carol's old room while her daughters would take turns sleeping on the fold-out couch in the downstairs living room.

Our sleep was shattered when the phone rang early the next morning. It was Aunt Carol. I heard dad tell Carol to calm down, get a hold of herself, and let him know what had happened. Dad and mom immediately dropped me off with a yawning sitter. Mother was softly crying. Dad, in a stunned shock, sped the car toward grandma's house.

Although I was just a small boy, everything soaked in. My parents tried to keep the more bizarre details from me, but snippets of conversation at Grandma Barnes' funeral helped fill in any blanks.

"...poor old girl. How could it have happened? She wasn't even sleeping in that room..."

"...found her in her closet. Carol said she was stark white, eyes wide with..."

"It was a massive heart attack, although I heard her mind was starting to..."

"...must've closed herself in, too. They said the doors were shut. Poor old girl..."

The Present

I don't like it when my wife goes away on business trips. This time she left me with what is rapidly becoming clear as much more than my imagination. Over thirty years have passed since that disturbing last visit to Grandma Barnes' house. I haven't thought much about it since. Perhaps I've

70

succeeded in vanquishing that dreadful afternoon from my consciousness. But as I lie here clutching my bed sheet, the memory rushes through me as though it had occurred only yesterday.

Mother always told me I'd inherited Grandma Barnes' graceful looks and charm. Unfortunately I don't think that's all I've inherited. I've heard talk that certain genes will skip a generation. Things like cancer, alcoholism, even Alzheimer's can be passed on down the family tree.

But now I know that there are other things...stranger, colder, sharper things that also get passed on down. The phone sits on the bedside table. If I wasn't frozen in fear, with my heart pounding so quickly, I'd reach for it. But call who? And say what?

The exhaling noises are getting louder now. Stronger. The scratching has ceased. At first I hoped, then prayed, that it was the moon coming in through the bedroom window and playing impossible tricks on me, but, oh dear God, dear God, the closet door is beginning to open...

The Bump-Bump Man

Dad's visits are a blessing. He plays with his granddaughters during the day, helps with dinner in the evening, and periodically baby-sits so that Beth and I can catch a movie or night out. Every summer since mom passed away he comes to stay with us for a month. I listened as dad told my little girls the same bedtime story he'd frightened me and sis with some twenty-five years earlier. The girls were wide-eyed with fright as dad gestured theatrically with his unlit pipe and spun that old, familiar yarn. My wife Beth looked concerned so I mouthed "Don't Worry" to her. If anything, dad's old spooky story has more relevance today then when I was an adolescent. I leaned back in my armchair and watched as my father continued.

"You must always lock your doors at night before you go to sleep," dad exaggerated in his mock dread voice. "Never forget to lock all your doors and windows, because in the wee, wee hours of the night, when you're off in sleepy-leepy land, the Bump-Bump Man comes a checking. He tries the front door first. If that's locked, the Bump-Bump Man will try the back door, a side entrance, and then the sliding glass door. Occasionally, in Summer months, he will check a window or two. And if the Bump-Bump Man finds an unlocked door or an open window, girls, he will come in to check on you, and you will suddenly find yourself eyeball to eyeball with a very unpleasant and unforgiving thing who does more than go bump in the night. I cannot tell you exactly what occurs when he gets in, girls, because it's unspeakable. What occurs when the Bump-Bump Man gets in is simply unspeakable." Dad pointed at his granddaughters with the stem of his pipe, "Promise me girls that you will always double check the doors and windows at night, and that you will never ever forget because the Bump-Bump Man always comes for a midnight check."

Dad then had the girls lock all the doors and windows before we retired for what dad had referred to as sleepy-leepy land. I thought about how that story had scared the pants off of me when I was growing up. In my mind's eye I could almost picture a tall and lonely shadow figure as he walked down endless midnight streets and cuts across blackened lawns in his silent pursuit of that one door handle which twisted and turned fatally inward. Subconsciously, through the years, I would check all the doors before going to sleep at night. In this day and age it just made good sense.

When I was a boy, there was a woman who lived behind us and further up the block who had been strangled to death one dark night. Her name was Mrs. Thompson. Mrs. Thompson was a divorcee who lived alone. The police eventually arrested her former husband. You know how that goes, bent love and codependency turned violent. If I recall correctly her ex-husband maintained his innocence throughout the entire trial but, then again, don't they all? Before they finally arrested her ex, I believed her death to be the grisly calling of the Bump-Bump Man, and that this poor, divorced woman had made the single, deadly error of leaving her door unlocked and an unspeakable thing had occurred.

I remembered how a couple living near my best boyhood friend, Bobby Venteer, had been killed in a burglary gone awry. My buddy Bobby made sure to give me all the gory details. The man had been bludgeoned with a lamp base. Evidently, Bobby had informed me, the man had been beaten beyond recognition while his wife had been strangled with an appliance cord taken from their kitchen. The police never found the killer. I remember telling Bobby, in all boyish sincerity, about how I felt it was the gruesome work of the Bump-Bump Man. Bobby laughed and playfully punched at my arm.

So this morning, when I wake to the sound of an ambulance and police cars rushing down the block, sounds seldom heard in this upper class suburb, the hair on the back of my neck begins to rise. I jog across several neighboring lawns to see if I can be of assistance. As a Medical Doctor I realize how on-the-spot treatment can save a life. It's the Bradley house. Out of breath I explain to the police that I'm both a neighbor and a doctor, and I've come to provide medical help.

An officer walks me up into the house. There was nothing I could do. Mr. Bradley had been bludgeoned to death. Mrs. Bradley had been strangled with a phone cord. Their seven-year-old son found them that way in their master bedroom. The officer who had walked me in tells me that the killer must have come in through the side door which, unfortunately, looks to have been left unlocked. The police are waiting for the coroner and some detectives from Homicide to arrive.

As I begin my short walk back home from the Bradley's, I almost step on it in the middle of their front yard. Suddenly I find myself remembering the father of my childhood. The father who played endless catch with me. The father who put me through medical school. The same father who tells one particular bedtime tale I'd always assumed fictitious.

And now, as I pretend to tie my shoe while stuffing the dew-soaked and familiar looking tobacco pipe into my pocket, I feel the lump swell deep in my throat. I love you Dad, always will, and I can never even begin to repay you for all that you've done for me. But, Dad, there's something I need to know... What have you been doing with your nights?

Clippings

To the Editor   The Fairmont Tribune July 17

As the senior member of the English faculty at Fairmont Junior High School, I am embarrassed at having to write this letter to the Fairmont Tribune. Am I to understand that you at the Tribune profess to employ writers with the grammatical skills necessary to construct two or more proper English sentences in succession? Be assured, Dear Editor, your syntax is purely and simply a joke.

Setting aside the numerous, generally infantile, run-on sentences strewn throughout your editorial of July 12, your incorrect use of the word "juxtaposed" did not fit the substance of your essay. Furthermore, your incorrect usage of the term makes your comparison between the Fairmont Sanitation Dump and the local water reservoir an oxymoron, and moot as well. Next time you feel the urge to use big words, for heaven's sake look up their meanings first.

In addition to misspelling Councilman Brenner's name, two N's, not one, you botched the fact that he was first elected in 1990, not 1992 as so mistakenly reported in your editorial. It's challenging enough to impart to my students the merits of correct writing skills without having such shoddy work appear almost daily in their hometown newspaper. You are in dire need of a proofreader, grammarian, and fact-finder. You should know there are numerous third graders from Fairmont Elementary I could confidently recommend.

Editor, Edit Thyself,

Abigail Millicent Tiddlesworth

Fairmont Woman Missing The Fairmont Tribune Aug 21

A Fairmont woman has been declared missing by the Fairmont Police Department today. Abigail Tiddlesworth was last seen by husband Leo Tiddlesworth Tuesday evening when she left home to go shopping. Police Chief Whitey Nelson told reporters that "at this time there is no reason to suspect foul play."

Mrs. Tiddlesworth has taught English in the Fairmont School District for thirty-six years and has been Chair of the...

To the Editor The Fairmont Tribune Sep 6

What sortta sport-hating kill-joy has your paper got working in its editorial department? Everyone agrees that cuts in the public school system's budget are needed, but why should the Athletic Department continue to take it on the chin—especially when spectator events like football and both boys' and girls' basketball draw so good as to practically pay for themselves, usually. But you're saying—quote—"we should fund math and humanities first." Righhhht, and exactly when was the last time you filled an auditorium with a Mathematics' quiz? Not a lot of popcorn sold at those Debate Club tournaments is there?

As a proud Tri-Captain of the Fairmont Cardinals' 1973 Season of Glory, I remember the townpeople and the press cheering us local boys all the way to a tie for District Runnerup. Nowadays, I'm surprised your paper has the stones even to cover the games from the home bleachers. Why should those of us who love spectator sports suffer because some pin-head editor who, if he won his letter at all in high school did it in sissified whining, has a personal vendetta against high school football? Just because yours have yet to drop, Mister Editor, doesn't mean you should ruin the fun for the rest of us.
Get a Clue, Bub,
Kevin "Buck" Lindstrom

Fairmont Man Found Beaten to Death
The Fairmont Tribune Oct 9

Kevin Lindstrom, 44, was found beaten to death in his garage Sunday evening by his ex-wife who had gone searching for him following his absence from their daughter's soccer scrimmage. A source within the police department told the Tribune that Lindstrom's face had been beaten so badly that his identity had to be confirmed through dental records. Robbery, at this point, does not appear to be the motive.

Although Fairmont Police have made no arrests, Police Chief Whitey Nelson held an impromptu press conference and told reporters his men are following up on several leads. Although Lindstrom's ex-wife described him as a "somewhat difficult man" to live with, she could not understand why anyone would have done this to him.

Lindstrom played left tackle on the 1973 Cardinal football team where Fairmont came within one field goal of winning the...

Letter to the Editor The Fairmont Tribune Oct 30

Bias most foul. Only members of the Politburo would cackle with glee to read your incessant leftist pabulum in the face of the staggering tax burdens already placed on the backs of the middle class. God forbid any truth gets in the way of your goose-stepping the party line.

Here's a helpful hint from Heloise – do your readership an enormous favor and slip a barf bag in between the pages of your Opinion section. That may save a bit of tidying up at the breakfast table.

Very Truly Yours,

Maria Tempell

Fairmont Woman Found in Dumpster
The Fairmont Tribune Nov 28

The charred body of a Fairmont woman was found in an alley dumpster by sanitation workers on their morning route Thursday. Maria Tempell was last seen leaving Dean's Tavern at about eleven o'clock Wednesday evening by bartender Pete Busin.

"Maria would come in a couple times a week for a nightcap. Sometimes she'd stay late talking politics with friends, but other times she was alone, like she was on Wednesday. Gosh," Busin told a Tribune reporter Thursday afternoon, "I sure hope this don't hurt business."

Police Chief Whitey Nelson, who has come under increasing criticism by members of the Fairmont City Council since the unsolved garage murder of Kevin Lindstrom early last October, had no comments on any specifics regarding the Tempell murder. But someone close to the Chief quoted him as saying he fears "Big city crime may finally have arrived in Fairmont."

Maria Tempell, a one-time Libertarian Party candidate for City Council, had long been involved with local politics and was responsible for...

Missing Teacher Found in Shallow Grave The Fairmont Tribune Dec 11

The remains of Abigail Tiddlesworth, longtime Fairmont English teacher who's been listed as missing since August 21, were discovered in a shallow grave by hunters in a wooded hollow near Gumsrud Creek. Police have repeatedly questioned her husband Leo Tiddlesworth since his wife's disappearance, but have yet to charge him.

Police Chief Whitey Nelson, who has been under constant demands from the Fairmont City Council to solve the garage murder of Kevin Lindstrom and the Dumpster death of Maria Tempell, continues to refuse to talk to the press. The triple homicides, occurring within a four month period, constitute more than Fairmont has seen in the past two decades. Fairmont residents, alarmed by recent developments, are wondering just what is happening in their fair city.

Although police officials will not speculate, many believe that these homicides are connected, and that the evidence points toward the work of a

76

serial or spree killer. Others believe that gang activity, heretofore unknown in Fairmont, may be the cause of...

A Short Note to Readers The Fairmont Tribune Dec 21
It is with great regret that we at the Tribune bid farewell to one of our own. Paul Elan, Fairmont Tribune's Editorial Page Editor is leaving us to work on the Omaha Stockman-Gazette. In the brief year that Paul has worked on the Tribune he has striven to give our editorial page great balance in dealing with the social concerns facing our community. As Paul leaves us to work for a bigger paper in a different state, we wish him the best of luck in all his future ventures. Punch and cookies will be served at...

Police Chief Nelson to Resign The Fairmont Tribune Jan 3
Police Chief Whitey Nelson delivered his resignation, effective immediately, to the Fairmont City Council on Tuesday, January 2. Although Chief Nelson has been with the Fairmont Police Department for eighteen years, he has come under wide criticism in recent months, by council members and others, for an inability to solve any of the three homicides that have haunted Fairmont since last fall. Long active in the Elk Lodge, Former Chief Nelson plans on moving his family to South Bisbee Junction, Arizona where he has accepted a position as Night Manager at the local bowling...

Body Found in Gully
The Omaha Stockman-Gazette March 2
A man's body was discovered in a gully near Highway 5 outside of Omaha late last night. Although the Omaha Police Department have yet to release the identification of the man, who is reported to have been badly beaten, they are following up a number of leads....

The Taming

"Good morning, distinguished scholars and learned guests. Welcome, welcome one and all. I want to thank you for attending the first of hopefully many Anti-Stratfordian conferences. I hope the luxurious accommodations of this conference center meet your every need. True, it's a little off the beaten path, but I think we all can enjoy a touch of seclusion now and again, kind of our island hideaway from the stress and strain of academia for a day or two. Of course, as I pointed out to several of you over morning coffee and Danish, given the huge grant from our anonymous benefactor, price is no object ... not anymore ... heh, heh, heh. (Laughter, applause.)

"If we haven't yet met, I'm Octavius Petruccio, Professor Emeritus of Elizabethan Literature, recently retired from the University of Verona. I imagine many of you in the audience are wondering why I, a traditional Shakespeare scholar, would found and be the first Keynote speaker at a conference which leans heavily toward Oxfordians, those who believe that it was *not* Will Shakespeare of Stratford-upon-Avon at all ... no siree, it was Edward de Vere, Seventeenth Earl of Oxford, who was the true Bard, the true author of these plays and sonnets we all love so much. Well, I thought it'd make for a fun weekend of debate. Perhaps I could bring some light and heat, stir the pot, if you will. I'm sure you'll enjoy the variety of breakout sessions that we've planned for today. And in that mode, we are most honored to have more than a dozen noted researchers here to share their most current data, feed the flames of discussion.

"Are there any Baconians in the audience? Those who regard Sir Francis Bacon as the true author? Raise your hands. Oh yes indeed, more than a few! Have we any pro-Marlowes in the crowd? I see a couple. Any Ben Johnsons? Sir Walter Raleighs? Not many. Any Queen Elizabeths out there? No, I thought not. Those have kind of gone the way of the pterodactyl, haven't they? And you Oxfordians raise your hands. My, my, my! The noble Earl appears to carry the day. (Applause.)

"Just out of mild curiosity, are there any traditional Shakespeare scholars like myself here today? No hands. Ahhhh me oh my, well, I didn't expect so. (Laughter.)

"I do see so many noteworthy intellectuals in the audience, and I do hope I get a chance to meet with each and every one of you as the breakout sessions progress. Why in the very front row is the esteemed Professor J. Callie Sanford, III—please stand and be recognized, Professor. I think most have read Professor Sanford's recent article in *Harper's* this past year. Edward de Vere himself would be proud of the case the good professor laid out. (Loud applause.)

"And there's the illustrious Darton Montaque sitting near the aisle. Up up up, Darton dear lad. Darton's rebuttal to my thesis on Shakespeare's knowledge of Italy certainly cut to the quick. But all in good fun ... heh heh heh. Yes, indeed. All in good fun.

"I know my favorite colleague and debate opponent, Doctor Katherine Tiltindanse, is here today, aren't you, Katherine? Let's see now, where are you? Yes. Hiding in back, huh? I suspect Professor Tiltindanse knew I'd be pointing her out as Katherine and I have done the circuit, as they say. What have we done, M'dear, brought our traveling discussion to nearly 30 colleges? I think that's about right. Sweet Kate's an excellent debater. Her sharp tongue has me against the ropes on nearly every campus. I am certainly delighted that you could be here today, M'dear. More than you'll ever know. (Cheers and clapping.)

"I'd also like to acknowledge and welcome all of our international colleagues, from England and the Continent, who were kind enough to jump the pond in order to be here today. We look forward to rubbing elbows with you, as it were, at the social engagements planned for the next two days.

"Most of today's breakout sessions are going to deal, in some depth, with the mystery surrounding Shakespeare's true identity. So I'd like to begin today with a quick overview of the Shakespeare establishment's stance, the viewpoint with which I am affiliated. If you could just bear with me for a few minutes, and keep the occasional hissing to a bare minimum ... heh, heh, heh ... I'll try to be brief.

"First, there's the debate surrounding Shakespeare's education. Anti-Stratfordians point out that there is no evidence of Shakespeare's schooling, no paper trail ... no grade lists for Latin or Greek, no graduation rolls, nada. But what they forget to utter is that there is no documentation of any student at the Stratford school during Shakespeare's lifetime. This lack of a paper trail does not make the Bard different from his contemporaries. Elizabethan playwrights who have no documentation of schooling include the poet Michael Drayton, the classical scholar George Chapman, as well as our good friend Ben

Johnson. I could go on and on, but I sense that eyes are beginning to glaze over.

"I'm sorry, what's that, Dear Kate? The entry doors are closed? Yes, we don't want any outside noise interrupting. Oh, I see, they appear to be locked. Oh, goodness, historic buildings like this one probably have some maintenance issues. I see that my assistant has already headed out the door behind the podium in answer to your concern. What's that, Darton old boy? Understood. Coffee goes right through me, too, just be patient. I'm sure it'll be resolved in just a few minutes.

"Let's see. Where was I? Oh yes, Oxfordians claim that the man from Stratford was actually a 'William Shaksper.' That's S – H – A – K – S – P – E – R. A man whose name was both spelled, and, yes learned colleagues, pronounced differently than that of the Bard himself, 'William Shakespeare.' Quite frankly, it would never have occurred to the people in 1600 to mix up the two.

"As you know, Professor Montaque is the second Keynote speaker. And I can see him chomping at the bit to get up here for rebuttal. The good professor is an *honorable* man, who'll no doubt correct my erroneous musings.

"Another Oxfordian assertion is that the true author of the plays had to have been a nobleman; an aristocrat well versed in the social order—the caste system—of the day. But Shakespeare scholars would point out that nobody in Shakespeare's day imagined that the plays displayed a true depiction of royal courts. Everyone knew the plays were fantasies of the great and mighty. It may make promoters of Edward de Vere cringe, but, dare I posit that most historians of Elizabethan times would stand on my side.

"Is that Professor Tiltindanse waving her hand back there? I believe we're saving Q and A for after lunch, M'dear. Plenty of time to make your points then, Sweet Kate. Nobody's ever accused Professor Tiltindanse of not having her fair say. No sir. Nobody would dare say that of Kate.

"In the spirit of full disclosure, I must confess that the Shakespearean establishment tends to think of Oxfordians as obstinate beasts, pit bulls if you will, immune to reason or any sense of decorum. I mean, honest-to-goodness, you certainly are dug in, aren't you? Endlessly mired in this bog of conspiracy, and spurred on by the ignoramuses in the press.

"I must admit that I get frustrated at times. I do, indeed. A little hot beneath the collar, as they say. After all, you're only discussing the greatest wordsmith in the history of letters.

"Huh? Yes, that is an interesting smell. I'm sure in an old building such as this, they use many industrial cleansers. Smells like what, Darton? Kerosene? Don't be silly, Old Lad. A bit too much Mr. Clean in the mop bucket, methinks.

"One thought to leave you with is how the Anti-Stratfordians strongly assert the early quartos of the Bard's plays did not have an author's name on them, implying that there was some grand scheme to keep the name secret. One needs to understand that only 30% of the plays printed in the 1590s named the author on the title page. And Shakespeare was establishing himself on the scene during those years. Did you know that Marlowe was never listed on a title page while he was alive? In fact, Marlowe was never mentioned as a playwright while he was alive. Perhaps the good Earl of Oxford also penned *Doctor Faustus* … heh, heh, heh. (Loud hissing.)

"What's that? I'm sorry I didn't quite hear you. Smoke. I don't really … hmmm, just a whiff. Perhaps some Walter Raleigh supporter is sneaking a cigarette. Tsk, tsk, tsk, Sir Walter. (Nervous laughter.)

"Distinguished guests, it appears that I've hit my allotted time. If you could please excuse me, I need to sneak out this back exit and take care of a final conference logistic. One last door for me to shut, if you will.

"I must thank you for being such a receptive audience, and I genuinely hope that you'll enjoy the remainder of the conference…"

The Forever Stone

Am I in a hospital bed?

I remember being distracted. Running late. Perhaps I stepped out into the street and was struck by a car? How long have I been out? My vision is blurred and I try to blink, but can't.

A face appears. It's Michelle. Enchanting as ever, Michelle is staring straight down at me and I know everything is going to be all right.

"I'm a moron in these matters, but can you tell me about what makes for a good diamond? I'm interested in quality, nothing but the best."

And, for about the first time when it came to financial burdens, I meant it. Michelle knew it was coming, both sets of parents knew it was coming, and I had known it was coming from that first day of college when she shot me a shy smile from across the Freshman Composition class almost five years ago.

"A diamond free of flaws is the highest quality, the purest mineral in the universe. You can see how nothing interrupts the passage of light through its eye — its facets," the owner of Forever Jewelry held one up for me to see. Forever came highly recommended from the director of Accounting, my boss, at work. Forever Jewelry was not a chain. It was owned by an aging hippy couple that personally made all the wedding bands in their store. They'd turned it into an art form, which was what I wanted for Michelle. Price was no object.

"Think about it, Rob—may I call you Rob?—think about it Rob. Most diamonds are cut round with a full 58 facets. If it's a good cut light is reflected from each facet and then dispersed through the top of the stone—giving it more sparkle—much like this one." Forever's owner held another one up to the light. "Poor cuts lose light through the bottom of the diamond and then, alas, the gem's poetry is lost."

I've spent the last half-decade trying to decipher the kind of sparkle and light Michelle kicks off. Beautiful women make me nervous, so imagine my surprise when I finally got up the nerve to ask her out to a movie and the answer came back in the affirmative. Harder yet to believe she said yes to subsequent requests for cups of coffee, study sessions, campus walks, and a first kiss.

"Some women at work have these huge stones." I scratched my cheek and tried to sound brighter than I was, "How does size factor in with a diamond's worth?"

"Size is really a matter of individual preference. Two diamonds of equal carat weights, you see, can have very different prices. All depending on their quality. It's really the work of a master cutter that allows the diamond to be cut in such a way as to permit the maximum poetry of light to be reflected." The owner's nose crinkled slightly, "Here at Forever Jewelry we don't sell the opaque trinkets that you see at the strip mall stores."

"Can you tell me a little more about this one?" With thumb and forefinger I took the one he'd been holding and placed it into my hand.

"This perfect diamond is what they call a round brilliant. It has the best angles and has been refined for the ultimate shine. This is a wonderfully cut piece. We call it our "Forever Stone.'"

I was still as giddy and goofy today when it came to Michelle as I had been in those first few months of courtship. Holding her hand cured the worst of days. Making her smile or tilt her head back and laugh in that little girl manner was everything, my everything. My life. *I'll always be with you*, I told her nightly, the last thing to say before drifting off to sleep, *I'll be with you forever, Michelle.*

"Can you put this stone into the matching wedding band? The one that we talked about for her?" I continued staring into the piece.

"I can do anything," he assured me.

Having spent my lunch at the jewelry store, I was running late. I had a 1:30 conference call with the Sur-Tel folks that, my being primary, Jack Moran would expect me to carry. The Sur-Tel account was fine, but they needed the usual client handholding. I promised the Forever' owner I'd be back the next day to dot all the i's and cross the t's.

I darted out of Forever and started jogging down Grand toward my car, parked a few hectic blocks away. I almost missed the cart that suddenly poked its nose in front of me from around the corner the building. I clipped it with my thigh and sent it toppling over sideways. I half turned and saw what I'd done. A grocery cart was on its side, tires still spinning. Contents were spilling out. Empty aluminum cans were rolling down the Fifth Street hill. Crumpled papers, Kleenex and what looked like yarn floated in the breeze.

I started back to help, but froze when I saw who had been pushing the cart. The old bag lady sat on the sidewalk, one bony hand still clutching the cart's handle, the other reaching out toward a floating piece of newspaper. She was a smear of filth and grime, with a leathery yellow face and a bird's nest of stark white hair—looking like the worst warted crony to have hobbled out of a Dickens' nightmare. And she stared up into my face—seeming ancient beyond belief.

I took another step toward her, to help her up, but stopped. Her stench of garlic, sweat, and rotting apples drifted over me. I tried not to gag. "I'm ... I'm sorry," I mumbled and resumed my sprint across the Grand and Fifth Street intersection.

When I got across, I turned back. I couldn't *not* help her, wasn't brought up that way. The Sur-Tel folks could wait. The bag lady was still sitting on the cobblestones where I'd accidentally knocked her down, but her free hand, the one not clutching the cart, was in the air and pointing at me. She marked me with her eyes, two dead marbles in a pool of white. Her lips twitched up and down in what appeared to be whispered profanity.

I started getting second thoughts about helping when her fingers slowly raised and I found myself staring almost hypnotically into her palm. I could see something there, something she wanted me to see—something she wanted to share. A scar—bright red—somehow burned deep into the center of her hand. It was mesmerizing, actually. Captivating. So deeply red. I wondered how it looked up close. Maybe if I could just get close enough to —

It must have been at that instant, wasn't it, that I stepped back into the intersection and got hit by a car?

Michelle's hair is cut short to her face, a different look. And I see lines about the eyes—lines that I may be responsible for. How the hell long have I been out? Next to Michelle is my good friend and colleague Jack Moran. I try to speak but nothing comes out. It slowly sinks in that I can't move a muscle while they gaze down at me. I must be heavily sedated or, God forbid ... paralyzed? I stare back, almost blinded by the glare of my vision.

"I'm oddly drawn to this one," Michelle's face has the familiar wrinkled look that I've seen a thousand times. The one she gets when making a big decision.

"It's gorgeous," I hear Jack exclaim.

"It's one of a kind." Another voice responds.

I recognized that last voice and was searching my memory when the graying jeweler leaned into view. Now why on earth would he be visiting me in the hospital? I suppose the accident happened right outside his door. Heck, he probably called the ambulance.

"That one's got a bit of a story to it," the jewelry storeowner looked at Michelle and Jack. "Some years back a gentleman commissioned me to make that for the love of his life. He never came back and I haven't seen him since, but the romantic in me kept hoping and hoping that someday he'd be back. Just this very morning I finally got around to taking it out of the safe and placing it on display."

"Guy probably got cold feet," Jack joked.

"Maybe, maybe not ... the fellow didn't seem the type," the storeowner mused. "Would you like to try it on?"

"May I?" Michelle asked softly.

"Of course, sweet lady, of course."

I don't understand. Am I in a coma? Are they visiting me in some dusty long-term care facility and making idle chitchat to pass the time. I see the owner begin to reach down toward me and ... Oh! ... *weightless I am lifted up... My! ... I have a kaleidoscope of eyes ... God! ... I can see in all directions.* Michelle and Jack are closer now, looking right at me, they're smiling.

"I love you, Michelle." Jack is talking now, "I guess I always have."

"I know you do, Jack..."

With many eyes I watch the glistening tear slip silently down Michelle's cheek.

"...I know you do."

I'm held in front of Michelle, swirling. Then, with one of my many eyes I spot her. I see her as she pauses outside of Forever's window. How could I forget that white nest of hair? Her dead marble eyes gaze into my lost soul. She's not quite human I sense, and as our paths once crossed dreadfully – neither am I. And I see with my now-great clarity the final bitter look the spell caster sends my way as she begins pushing her cart of empty soup cans and other found things past the jewelry shop.

"It's been almost three years, Michelle," Jack is trying to close the deal, "and you and I both know he'd want you to get on with your life. I'll be a good husband, Michelle. I'll take care of you."

"I know, Jack. And you've been so very good to me these past years." Michelle continues staring down at me. "It's so...so... It seems made for me. May I pick this ring?"

"I couldn't think of a better one for you."

Although I no longer have a mind, I think of the many years ahead that'll unfold for you and Jack, and for your children and grandchildren. The heart I no longer have breaks in two. My three score of eyes, which can never weep, now stream tears of light.

I always swore I'd be with you forever, Michelle ... and it appears I'm going to get my wish.

The Ten O'Clockers

"So I picked up the football and ran it all the way back for a touchdown. Eighty six yards. It was out of pure impulse."

"Pure impulse?"

"Well, even then I was a big lump, all thumbs and left feet. It got stripped from Hamden's quarterback before he hit the ground. A bunch of us were standing around thinking the play was dead and I just happened to be the one to pick it up and run." Donovan smiled as if in apology for confessing his shining moment from boyhood. "If not for a that impulsive move, completely unplanned and unthinking, I wouldn't have a favorite high school memory.

"I know the feeling, Donny, now and then after I fill the gas tank I get a sudden impulse, what the hell, as long as I'm standing here paying the cashier maybe I really do need a kingsize bag of those peanut M&Ms they have sitting out."

"Exactly. An impulse item. Something that nine times out of ten, you wouldn't do, but somehow it flashes through you. In half a nanosecond. And you must do it."

"A reflex reaction."

"Like some warped magnetic pull that you're powerless against, Jim."

"Can I blame a warped magnetic pull for my first marriage?" I asked.

"Not unless both you and she just happened to be in Vegas and the two of you just happened to walk past a wedding chapel." Donny's voice dripped sarcasm.

"Guess I can't blame that one on impulse."

"Blame horniness."

"Hey, I was young." I looked across the table at Donavan. It was our first day back in the old routine. "The Ten O'Clockers, back by popular demand. I know it's wrong to speak ill of the – you know – but these breaks are actually pleasant again. Just like old times."

"Ain't that the sad truth."

"What do you suppose he was thinking?" I asked in a whisper.

"Probably wondering if thirty stories up gave him enough time to learn to fly."

At Chad Erickson's funeral, the pastor asked if anyone would like to stand by the closed casket and say a few words. Donovan nudged me in the ribs with his elbow. I stifled a grimace. What could I possibly have to say about Erickson? *Ladies and gentlemen, my name is Jim Bartlett. I worked with Chad at Posi-Tech. And I'd like to think he meant well. Thank you for listening. Goodbye.* Fortunately, a couple of his siblings stood up and got the job done.

I'd been working at Posi-Tech Engineering for almost eight years. Donovan had me beat by two months and some change. I helped write the code for a variety of Posi-Tech's software applications. Donovan, a mechanical engineer, worked in Quality Control. Our paths had crossed frequently that first year and we hit it off. Similar age, similar interests, same generation. I barely remember when we first started taking our Ten O'Clockers in the cafeteria, had to be some years before the remodeling started.

I always got to the Posi-Tech Tower before seven to beat morning rush hour, hit it hard for a few, and then have a pre-lunch break with my confidant. I hang back while Donny grabs a cup of java and a Danish – or a juice or maybe a banana, and buys them from the Register Hag. The Hag once caught me lifting some of the cafeterias plastic forks for use with my home-brought fruit cup, and, by the time she got done gnawing on my ankle bone – I thought I'd need a rabies shot. Not that I'm uniquely afraid of the Hag because if push comes to shove, everybody's afraid of the Register Hag.

Once past the Hag, Donny 'n I'd grab our favorite table by the window and shoot the breeze for twenty minutes. Banter, shovel B.S., exchange office gossip, blow off steam … I think you get the point.

Truth be known, breaks with Donny were my favorite part of the workday. His wry sense of humor and easy willingness to listen helped me get through the emotional shards of a messy divorce, of quitting the habit, of missed promotions, and of countless other curveballs. Hopefully, the feeling was reciprocated.

Along came Chad Erickson. He'd first been brought aboard as a contractor back in the days we were sweating the Y2K recoding. I'd met him on the periphery of several of my projects. Our relationship evolved from the obligatory nod in the hallway to a passing exchange of small talk by the water fountains to an occasional e-mail joke. Evidently, Erickson's work cut mustard and they hired him on permanently. I even remember shooting him off a congratulatory e-mail.

Early last year was my regrettable faux pas. I'm the one who introduced Erickson to Donovan (and I'm not sure he's ever forgiven me). Being territorial beasts, Donny and I were sitting at our usual table telling lies about women while looking out over the city. Chad Erickson happened past carrying an assorted mess of food - a bag of Doritos, a big box of Junior

Mints, and a pair of 16-ounce Pepsi that he'd just pulled from the vending machines.

"Geeze, Chad. You must have mortgaged the house to buy all those carbs."

"Well, what's a morning without washing down my Junior Mints with a couple large Pepsi Colas?" he said loudly as he pulled over an empty chair.

"Chad, I'd like to introduce you to…"

"Actually, I dip the Doritos in the Junior Mints," Erickson chortled, his cheeks bright red.

"Now that would make for an interesting taste. Have you met…"

"…but then again maybe I'll pour the mints and the Doritos into a bowl and use the Pepsi for milk. It's close enough to breakfast the most important meal of the day."

"Pete," Pete was Donovan's first name, not that it ever got much play. "I'd like you to meet Chad Erickson who…"

"…or maybe the Dorito mints could be for brunch since, like I mean it is close enough to lunch."

It took me about five minutes to wedge into Chad's nonstop yammering an introduction to Donny, who seemed good-naturedly amused by my struggle. Our morning skies quickly darkened. Chad invited himself to our Ten O'Clockers. The thing I learned about Erickson was, in small doses, he could be digested. In large doses, meaning two minutes or more of listening to his marathon of trivial chatter, was like ingesting fiberglass. What Chad lacked in wit he made up for in decibel. Within two weeks I considered sending my resume to out-of-state recruiters, so I wouldn't have to be in the same city with the perpetual motor mouth.

Maybe if there was real humor buried in the blather but … well, you judge. On one occasion Donovan had to run to a meeting right after break, so he happened to have a pen in his front pocket.

"So you're pen in pocket, today, huh, Donny?" Erickson heard me call Donovan 'Donny' once and he was off to the races. "I used to have pens in my pocket in junior high, Donny, but my red one broke and guess what…?" Followed by 18 minutes of Chad's loud, rambling guffaws about ink stained shirts, red blotches resembling chest wounds, and endless memories of knee-slapping eighth grade pantomimes of faked gunshot hits.

The next day it was Chad's philosophy of office memos triggered by a memo regarding a department meeting "So, Donny, you're Mr. Notetaking guy, today."

"I'll probably jot down stuff on the agenda."

"Agendamania has struck Posi-Tech again. Don't you just wonder how many trees they cut down to print agendas and yet everyone tosses them away because..."

"Say, Donny..." I attempted to squeeze a change of subject in edgewise. Futile.

"They should write the agenda on the white board. Hey, you ever smell the markers that go with those white boards? Some have scented flavors. Grape's my favorite." Erickson shook his head like a bobble doll. "Now it'd be worse to have one of those nasty things break in your pocket. Boy, there'd be a real mess and you can just bet your skin would be tinted."

On another occasion I had a minor case of the sniffles.

"Going to cruise through a big box of Kleenex today, huh, Jimmy Boy?"

"I'm hoping the Sudafed will..."

"...while everybody says where's Jim?" Chad Erickson cut me off. "I'll tell 'em I last saw him down in the boiler room sneezing into the ventilation shaft sharing his virus-packed spittle with everyone in the building." Chad paused and tittered with delight as he wiped a tear from his eye, "So you can make us all sick, right, Jimmy Boy?"

And on and on it went, daily, with Chad as our personal tour guide through the seven outer rings of hell. Donny and I would trudge back to work every morning at twenty past ten numb and peevish, dead about the eyes, looking as though we'd joined the Bataan Death March and feeling as though we'd been through shock treatment, which, in effect, we had.

"What's the saying, Jim?" Donny called my office after one particularly exasperating break of interruptions and bad jokes. "We're suffering a fool."

"But not gladly," came my feeble response. "I wonder if the guy's got an off button."

As a defensive tactic Donny and I tried to vary our break times, sometimes at 9:30, others at 10:30. But within a day there'd be Chad, looking like some lost mutt who'd found his way home, beaming at us with his loud, goofy smile and complete lack of self-awareness. Donny and I figured that Chad Erickson must sprint by our offices and, if we weren't in, beeline it for the cafeteria to dazzle us with his verbal brilliance.

After playing games for an agonizing month, Donny and I tossed in the towel. No more Ten O'Clockers. Work was more enjoyable than listening to Erickson's stream-of-consciousness babble as he rubbed his red cheeks and paused long enough to gulp air before he'd railroad over our sentences. It was sapping our life marrow. If Erickson ignored not ever having been invited to join us, as well as missing the subtle nuances of our switching break times on him—then nothing would sink in.

Donny and I gutlessly decided to give up our breaks rather than have what would have been an uncomfortable come-to-Jesus conversation with Erickson. When Chad stopped by that first week or so, we'd tell him no break due to meetings or demanding projects. I even mumbled something to him about my boss starting to monitor my time. And that's how The Ten O'Clockers were dropped altogether.

Over saddened beers one Friday night, Donny told me his parlor psychiatry held that Chad Erickson was obviously a needy sort who desperately craved attention. I concurred. Donny figured whatever nut patch family Chad'd been raised in, they'd amputated all the guy's normal sensibility and he honestly wasn't even aware of his being such an irritant. For Erickson to exist, Donny posited, he had to shut down the part of his consciousness that would make him aware that he was, most definitely, a boob. The annoying sap was actually kind of pathetic. No real friends, and a lifetime of acquaintances doing their darndest to avoid him.

On the day of Chad Erickson's plummet, the maintenance man had slipped away to the bathroom and couldn't have been gone ten minutes – perhaps a little longer if he washed his hands. But he'd left the cones out, and the opening was less than three feet. And for crying out loud, the repairman likely told the public hearing, the east bank of elevators had been closed all week.

Posi-Tech was housed with a handful of other companies in the Posi-Tech Tower building; 42 floors of glass. In order to modernize the Posi-Tech Tower, which had been built in the late 1960s, the building management company had put in place some rather grandiose plans – a facelift with all the trimmings. Posi-Tech's rent would likely skyrocket at the end of our current lease. The cafeteria had been remodeled (alas, the Hag remained), they had added a garden walk in the courtyard, the lobby was getting a complete makeover, new carpet springing up everywhere, and, in the last month, they had been adding a new electrical system to the elevators.

As part of the elevator revamping, they'd close off one side to transportation for a week, while they worked on that particular row of elevators. It would triple your wait time for the working bank of elevators when coming or going, but when you work on the 32nd floor – what are you gonna do? Sometimes, on the side that was shut for repair, the door would be open with the elevator car up two or three feet. Employees would walk by and sneak a quick look down the elevator shaft to see if it was like they show in the action movies. I'd even once knelt by the cones the maintenance crew had set up as a warning barrier in order to get a better look. It was out of some childish curiosity, like a boy peering down from his new tree house. I wondered if Erickson had felt that childish curiosity and had been drawn closer, and closer still.

The police didn't openly say it was a suicide – not in so many words anyway – but that could be out of respect for the family. Conventional wisdom had it that Chad lost his footing or tried to grab something as he squatted dangerously near the opening and slipped, but I wondered about that, too. Either way I imagined that Erickson's parents, as Chad wasn't married, would ultimately receive a sizable settlement.

"You know that feeling you get when you're standing on a bridge or a tower," Donny and I were now heading back up to work and I'd been meaning to bounce this thought off him, "and you're peeking over the edge, deep into the abyss, and you get that certain 'Why the F Not' feeling. I mean it would be so easy to just do it, but then you jerk back, giggle a little, and then go on with your life. Maybe something like that happened, only Chad didn't pull back."

"That impulse thing, huh?"

"Well. Let's say you're going over the waterfall before you know you even jumped, and by then you can't take it back no matter what."

"Maybe, Jim. But then again," Donovan took a last slow sip of his coffee, "then again maybe something else. Maybe you're standing on that ledge, but you're not alone. Someone is next to you, also staring into the abyss." Donovan's finger hovered toward the elevator button for several seconds before he pressed it. "And you find yourself looking over at him, watching him gaze downward, wondering what goes on in that content-free mind of his, and at that moment in time there's no one else in the world – just the two of you. And you feel that strange magnetic pull. And you are powerless. So you ..." Donny looked into my eyes as though searching for an answer, "... pick up the ball and run..."

I stared speechlessly at Donovan.

Somewhere in the background an elevator door chimed.

With One Magic Word

"I'm so cold, doctor. So very, very cold."

"Is it Billy I'm talking to now?" The bushy-browed Doctor Sivanna queried.

"Yes, doctor. It's me. It's Billy."

"Billy, I'm here to help you … I really am. We need to talk again."

"Don't leave me anymore, doctor. I'm so all alone. So alone and cold."

"I'm going to do everything I can to help you. You must trust me, Billy; trust me with the whole story. You know that, don't you, Billy?"

"I know that, doctor."

"Now let's talk again about the man. The stranger that first approached you that night all those years ago. The one who lured you down into the abandoned subway tunnel. Do you remember what he looked like?"

"Tall, dark trench coat and hat covering his face. He was a shadow, doctor. I couldn't see him, but I remember his breath. His breath smelled of death."

"Now, Billy, did this tall stranger, uh, touch you in any way?"

"He yanked my arm. There was something in the subway that he wanted me to see. He wouldn't let go."

"Did he touch you anywhere else?"

"Oh no, doctor, no. He just led me to the sorcerer. Then vanished like smoke up a chimney."

"The sorcerer?"

"He's the one who did this to me. I haven't seen him since. He's long gone, doctor. Dead, I think. Crushed. But the others … they hate me. I hear their voices. They think it's my fault. They want me dead, doctor. They want me dead." Billy stared into the doctor's eyes, "And I deserve it."

"Why do you deserve it, Billy?"

"My fault, all my fault. That's what they think."

"What do they think is your fault?"

"The change into the other." The tears rolled down Billy's face, "He's ruined my life."

"Let's talk about this sorcerer. What was his name again?"

"I can't… You know I can't say his name. I'll never say it again. No one'll ever make me say that word. Never again, doctor. I'll die first." Billy Batson wiped his eyes on his sleeve.

"Wasn't his name some kind of acronym? Made up of other names? Superman, Hercules, Atlas, Zeus, Achilles and—"

"Solomon. Not Superman."

"Of course," The doctor checked his notes. "Now when you say this acronym out loud the, uhhh, transformation occurs…?"

"Right. A blinding light and then … I'm there."

"Tell me, Billy, where do you go during the transformation?"

"A dark place. A nightmare of darkness—and it's cold. Damp. And I get so very frightened. The voices are getting stronger when I'm there, doctor. They know I'm there with them … and they want me dead. Doctor, they're going to kill me!"

"Billy, it's going to be all right, son. Trust me. Now I'm going to have to chat with—"

"Oh no, doctor. No! Don't go away, don't leave me!" Billy sobbed violently, his chest heaving. "Don't leave me again!"

"Shazam." Doctor Sivanna whispered the command and Billy's head lulled against his chest. "Now, I'd like to talk to one of the others. When I say the magic word, I'd like to talk with the other called Solomon. Three, two, one … Shazam."

Billy's head shot up. His now ancient eyes, green and piercing, took in the empty room, the buckled leather restraints, and the thickly padded walls before settling on the doctor. The ghost of a smile crossed Billy's lips, "So it's you again."

"Sir. I know you find our sessions somewhat tedious, but we need to know—"

"Shall we stop the games, doctor?"

"Sir, I'm trying to help the boy, little Billy. For a long time I thought you and the others were merely Billy's delusions. Until I tried the drugs and hypnosis. Learned how wrong I'd been about … all of you. Now I must help the boy."

"You're nothing more than an ointment, doctor, a lubricant. You're only needed to salve the little one's wounds so that he may be used again and again by your military."

"But look at the terrible thing you and the others are attempting to do. You're trying to make him commit suicide."

"Hmm." A fleeting grin flickered beneath the piercing ancient eyes. "It took awhile, lord knows that you were of no help, but we've figured things out now. We know it's because of him. And once that boy is gone, all this imbecilic turmoil ceases."

93

"How can you say such things?" the doctor tried another tact. "What the Captain does is good. He fights evil. My God, man, he's saved the planet time and time again."

"Don't be so naïve, doctor. Marvel has been a pawn of a corrupt government for years."

"That's simply not true." Doctor Sivanna paused, "We only want what's best for Billy."

"Don't bore me, doctor. You keep him heavily sedated and," the piercing eyes warily scanned the room again, "away from any sharp objects. Then you plunk him down in the middle of some overproduced psychodrama and coerce him into mumbling that which summons the Captain in all his big, red dimness."

"But you're from that same place. You come here from wherever that place is."

"Wrong as usual, Sivanna. I'm dozing in the restful mists of Valhalla when all of a sudden, in the blink of an eye, I'm yanked to wakefulness. Hurled to Earth in the guise of that costumed freak with the big biceps with five bi-polar neurotics vying for control … and that sobbing brat in the background makes it impossible to think."

"But you, and the others, you function together as Captain Marvel. We've all seen it time and time again."

"You call that functioning, doctor? Not by half. Every time the transformation happens, there's some lethal danger, something nasty demanding our utmost attention – just a big happy picnic, doctor? A stroll in the garden, huh? How would you like it if you got ripped to wakefulness from a deep slumber? Torn from the ancient mists and forced to confront flying alligators or Venus death beams, a division of blood- lusting troops, or some other costumed freak with a homoerotic motif trying to—what's that they say nowadays? 'pop a cap in your ass.' No tranquility, no time to pass 'Go'— no time to collect your two hundred dollars. And barely enough time to grab those flying gators by the balls before they rip your head off. You try living that way week after week."

"I sense your anger."

"I've got an ulcer the size of Mount Sinai. Say the magic word and there I am—crammed into tights and cape like sardines in a can with those other five muscle-bound lunatics. For Chrissakes, I dare you to talk with Achilles. Did you know that after we put the kibosh on the werewolf zombies from Atlantis, Achilles begged to go on a killing spree? That Greek's a psychotic bent on genocide, just like he did to Troy. Bring him forth for a quick palaver and he'd find a way to gnaw on your skull. Hard to blame him, what with all of Mercury's carping and Hercules's endless farts—now that one belongs in a stable—don't even get me started on Hercules!"

"Look, let's talk about Billy. Can you explain the transformation?"

"You're changing the subject, doctor. You didn't think Zeus and I would eventually piece this charade together, did you? The boy is the key. Plato was right, everything is becoming not being. From its essence … putting it in terms even you can understand, doctor, Billy is the pupa, the chrysalis, whose metamorphosis into Captain Marvel must be stopped. Billy must die."

"But Billy's done nothing. Please, Solomon, I implore you. Billy's just a little boy. A victim. Trapped just as surely as yourself. And the others. Given a little more time I think I can change all that."

"Stop playing God, that job's taken. So just get off it, doctor, you're messing with the natural outcome of this terrible thing, with Billy's fate. We're determined to save ourselves. As for you, doctor, go whistle *The Blue Danube* for all we care. And as for Billy, once we get the how-to's figured out, it'll be a mercy killing."

"We never get beyond this." Doctor Sivanna rubbed hard at his temples. "Shazam." Billy's head lulled against his chest.

"I need Billy again." The doctor collected his thoughts. "Shazam."

The pale, trembling newsboy opened his wet, fear-filled eyes. "Doctor, you left me again. You said you weren't gonna leave me. I've been so cold and alone."

"Billy, I'm here for you. You know that. I'll do anything I can. But first, something's come up. There've been threatening troop movements among that army of fanged Venusians … and we may need your help…"

Grog's Last Prank

"Avast ye scum-swabbing titmice," Johnny 'Grog' McRae stuffed the flashlight into the pocket of his green and gold school jacket. "Before I depart, land-lubbers, let me leave you with this."

"Oh no." Chip Davitt pinched his nose.

Grog let one rip. It echoed like a shotgun in the cavern. Smiling, he paused a second, then leapt from the edge of the enlarged row boat, over a few feet of oily water, and onto the simulated cave floor. The pervasive stench ought to give his fellow frat brothers something to mull over during the remaining minutes of their boat ride through the tacky amusement park's Ghost Pirates of the Red Cavern.

Grog raced toward a couple of mannequins dressed as pirate wenches. He put his arm around the scraggiest-looking harlot, cupped a breast with his left hand, and popped a sixteen ounce can of malt liquor with his right.

"Yo-Ho-Ho and a bottle of rum," Grog sang bawdily as he watched the boat turn a bend and disappear from view.

His gang of accomplices from Phi Delta Phi had tested the Ghost Pirates boat ride several times during the day, scoping it out, trying to locate where the best point would be for Grog to jump ashore. Each bend would display a different scene of cut-rate Long John Silvers plying their trade. There were plenty of seafaring mates with cutlasses in belts about the waist, ramshackle inns, shipwrecks, plank walkers, dynamite barrels, bottles of rum, damsel's in distress, and pirate wenches. Many more drunken buccaneers, cutthroats standing guard over trunks full of booty, railguns, battle settings on ship with marlinespikes, flintlock pistols, musketoons, and boarding axes. All displays, shown turn after twist in the makeshift river to theme music, culminated in the final ghost ship that hovers over you right before the final bend and exit out into the light.

This was going to be classic. He and Chip 'Chiparoo' Davitt had devised this latest prank. A prank to top all previous pranks. A prank that was bound to make the papers. A prank that would be the crown jewel in Grog's collection of stunts and practical jokes that he'd pulled in his 5-year tour of duty to receive a Business degree at Capwood College—green and gold forever. This prank would outshine the horse dung they'd taken from the Agriculture campus, made into relatively pleasant-looking sandwiches, burritos and stuffed cream rolls, wrapped them individually in cellophane, then snuck into the faculty's lounge overnight and refilled the vending machines. This current prank would even outdo the condoms they'd blown up with helium and distributed, en mass, during homecoming week. This prank was gutsier than when he'd switched labels on the Home Ec tape with a video from his Johnny-the-Wad collection, then took the batteries out of the Home Ec lecturer's remote control. The class got two minutes of something that wouldn't be appearing on any mid-term before the bowlegged ditz of a teacher finally figured out that she could stop the film by yanking the cord out of the socket. This would even be better than his all time personal favorite of sneaking into the campus theater the night before Capwood College's fall premiere of the play "Hello Dolly," and taking the set and backdrop apart screw-by-screw, nail-by-nail. In short order, he and a handful of other Phi Deltas had dismantled, and stacked neatly in back, what had taken the stage crew five weeks to build.

Grog and company had, earlier in the day, killed time by looking at the blazingly colorful pictures of the more infamous pirates, buccaneers, and privateers, which were framed outside the amusement park's river shack in order to draw passers-by inside. Each picture contained a short biography written in a campy, over-the-top manner. Those pictured included Bartholomew Roberts, Henry Morgan, Sir Francis Drake, Jacques LaRougue, perhaps better known as "The Red Jackal" by the pirate-plagued British merchant fleet, and, of course, the dreaded Blackbeard—scourge of the sea. Blackbeard, Chip Davitt's personal favorite, would, before battle, light slow-burning cannon wicks beneath his black hat so that there was always smoke whirling around his face. He met a bloody end in November of 1718 after being captured by the English Royal Navy. Blackbeard demanded hand-to-hand combat. It took 20 cutlass thrusts and five gunshots to kill him. British forces then brought Blackbeard's head back to Virginia, swinging wildly from the bow of their ship.

But the pirate that most caught Grog's imagination was "Calico Jack" Rackham. Tall and menacing, Rackham was nicknamed "Calico Jack" due to the calico britches and coat he often wore. Rackham, a merciless thief, had been known to do terrible, grisly, and quite intrusive things with his razor-sharp cutlass to captives, betrayers and a variety of other enemies. His pirate ship, *Revenge*, was caught by the British in 1720. Calico Jack was hung in Jamaica of that very same year. Calico Jack's pair of seafaring wives, Mary Read and Anne Bonny, wench pirates who'd held their own in many a maritime battle, were spared the noose as both were pregnant with Rackham's seed. Myth has it that at the same time Calico Jack swung kicking at the end of the hangman's rope; Read and Bonny went into labor.

Getting aboard the final boat ride of the evening had been easy. The Phi Delts waited outside until the line died down, and it was time to close for the night. The only employee in sight was a little guy who helped people get into the overlong row boats, which, on tracks beneath the water's surface, would pull them through the cavern.

"My watch says a minute to, kid," Grog lied as his six-two, 220 pound frame towered over the kid who ran the ride. Grog did his best not to snicker. The liquor he'd already ingested sure didn't help. On all previous passes, Grog had been positive that the boy was wearing makeup as to fit in with the spirit of the ride. But up close he could see that the poor guy had a dark, pimply complexion that looked to Grog like one of those Gypsy goat-boys who helped out Quasimodo in those bad, old black and white movies he'd skip class and drink to in the Phi Delta house's basement TV lounge. The boy, who couldn't be more than twelve, looked up at Grog with uncertainty.

"Didn't I drop enough candy in your bag last Halloween." As he said it Grog heard his fellow Phi Delts stifling their laughter. "C'mon, little fella, I'll get you some caulk for your face."

Grog's intimidation appeared to do the trick as the pimply goat-boy had paused for a long second, then reached behind him and unhooked the divider rope. He motioned them through and into the rigged row boat with his slender, pale fingers. As Grog passed, the boy gave him a crooked smile. Grog was taken aback to see little brown teeth, with gaps in places where you could slide a nickel upright.

"Jesus, kid, strike for Dental," Grog had hurried by and jumped into the back of the boat.

And now he stood inside the cavern. Alone. Sadly sobering up. And a bit spooked. Who wouldn't be? Ghost Pirates of the Red Cavern had water-level lanterns that gave the mannequins a sinister look. Grog walked over to a back corner and sat down on the sand. They must shovel buckets of sand over the plywood for full affect, he thought. He sipped from his malt liquor.

This crown jewel prank would even surpass his pickle jar full of the panties he'd stolen from his overnight conquests at a variety of kegger parties. *Gee*, Grog would say in the morning, or, perhaps an hour later, *I remember us taking them off by the door—hey, my mom's gonna be here any second. Put your pants on and I'll get them to you later.* And another pair of panties went into the pickle jar he'd have in the corner of his room hidden behind his entertainment unit. When just the boys were around, he'd haul the pickel jar out for a quick count. And so what if he would occasionally knick a pair or two from his sister's drawer when he went home for the holidays, and add them to his pickle jar collection? He was, after all, Grog, a.k.a. the Grogster, a.k.a. the Grogmeister, a.k.a. Fuckin'-A Party Dude, a legend, a living legend in the Phi Delta Phi at Capwood College.

Grog was going to miss the old green and gold. He loved Capwood, but, sadly, all good things must come to an end. Once he graduated and went out into the work world, people would expect him to show up at places before ten in the friggin morning. And he certainly wouldn't be known as "Grog" by any work colleagues. And he sure as hell wouldn't be able to pull ninety-nine percent of the crap he did at Capwood. He hadn't demanded much of college—a paper thin 2.5 GPA was quite okay with Grog, especially since he had a team of four-eyed sycophants churning out the major papers for him. He even gave his team strict instructions to not outright ace anything as to arouse suspicion, too dangerous, especially in them goddamned small classes where the professors get to personally know you and that sorta shit. However, the bigger sized classes, where you had stadium seating, were Grog's bread and butter. He had his flunkies exceed for him in those.

Grog grinned and downed some more malt liquor. Pretty soon goat-boy would turn off both the lights and the increasingly grating theme music. Then Grog'd wait a few minutes so that goat-boy could head off to his room, trailer, stable, or wherever it was goat-boy called home for a quick yank on his rip-cord and a night's sleep before the amusement park had him out bright and early to sweep up the cigarette butts, ticket stubs, and barf. Yup, in a half hour or so, Grog would be venturing into uncharted territory. He'd spent most of the week going through his frat's collection of Penthouse and Hustler in order to find a myriad of interesting positions. Chiparoo had even passed along a couple of drawings from the Kama Sutra. Jesus, it would be el pranko supreme when he got through. Tonight, Grog was going to rearrange the silly-ass mannequins in the pirate displays to look like something triple X-rated from one of Caligula's toga parties. Up the Jolly Roger would have new meaning. Grog would have Blackbeard doing Long John Silver from behind. He'd stage Henry Morgan having menois-a-dog, jail maties with guards, harlots, damsels and pirate wenches joined in a coital bliss that would make Larry Flynt proud; a surplus of exciting new positions for swords and sheaths. He'd even bring them fake alligators into the mix. Grog'd do it up right. Hell, he'd have all night.

Then, in the morning, Chip and the crew of Phi Delts would come through in the first boat. After a couple of bird call signals, Grog would pop back into the boat, and history would thus be made. One of the pledges would capture his work on video tape. Hopefully, tourists with kids, tiny ice-cream eating boys and girls, would take a morning Ghost Pirates of the Red Cavern ride. Goat-boy wouldn't have a clue, wouldn't know what to do, and would keep sending family after family on through until a posse of red-faced parents hunted down the park manager. Grog'd phone the media, make certain the story made the paper. Then he'd frame the article over the fire mantel at the frat house.

There really was no downside. If he got caught, he'd go O.J. and deny everything. Chip's dad owned a string of motels, and appreciated a good chuckle his ownself. Chip could always get his family's attorney to muddy the water, and, hell ya, even suggest that the goat-boy did it. *Your Honor*, Grog pictured himself standing, suited, tied, and straight-faced, before a judge, *I didn't want to bring this up, because we all have to be sensitive about these issues, but the kid had his back to us, and was doing something with himself down there. He zipped it up when he heard us step onto the boat launch.*

Grog heard a loud clanking noise and the overhead spotlights, used to showcase animated pirates, those swinging bottles of rum, those waving broad swords at the passing boats, those stroke-lighting cannons, or steering the helm of the ghost ship at the tunnel's end, all of them went out. A second later the annoying theme music ceased. Near darkness now shrouded Grog. Fortunately the water lanterns stayed on, giving off an eerie yellow, half-haze of light. Grog hung onto his flashlight, and waited a few minutes to accustom his eyes time to the dark.

Okay, he thought, first things first—time to leak the lizard. Grog sauntered over to the water, stood in the shadows away from the nearest water lantern, unzipped, and took out little Grog. An odd case of stage fright overtook him. C'mon, piss little Grog, let's get going. Grog snapped his head up. What the heck was that noise? It sounded like a muffled splashing sound. Something was in the water. Little Grog turtled inside the fly, and big Grog simultaneously took a step back while zipping. Taking a leak could wait.

What the hell was in the water? The sight of those rubber alligators, whose mouths opened wide revealing jagged teeth whenever a boat came near, flashed through Grog's mind. Could some final electricity still be working its way through those mechanical devices? How 'bout dogs? Maybe they let loose a couple of Dobermans in here for after hours security. Great—now I'll get bit on the ass by one of them. But wouldn't the dogs start barking if they sensed his presence? And would the theme park owners want guard dogs chewing up their displays, teething on the mannequins—or swimming in the dark muck for that matter? This prefab river, with whatever oils and grease they use for the boat tracks, would have to be polluted as all hell.

Then a thought occurred to Grog that made heap more sense. Rats. Carny rats as big as spaniels. Those rodents probably come in here looking for food or some other shit to gnaw on. Grog shivered. He'd only worn his college jacket, Jean shorts, and an old pair of Nikes because he figured he'd get wet up to his thighs bouncing from one bend in the makeshift river to another in order to rearrange the various displays.

The water sounds were louder, getting closer, just down river from him. If they have rodents, they also have cats in here to keep the population down, he'd seen a couple of scraggly-looking felines outside earlier in the day. That would be the smart thing to do. A bit unnerved, Grog took a giant step backwards and…something touched his back. Grog whirled about, a dark shape stood before him. Adrenaline and reflex took over. Both of Grog's hands shot forward, palms up, and pushed at the body with all his strength. The dark figure shot backwards. Upon hitting the ground, it lay there motionless. Grog held his boxer's stance as though saying, *C'mon prick, I'm ready for you now.*

The figure lay still, several feet from Grog, lying on its back. Grog fished the flashlight out of his pocket, and shone it on the ground before him. The pirate mannequin looked like some grotesque version of Smead from "Peter Pan"—only not smiling and with blood-red lips. Grog felt his muscles begin to unclench. He didn't remember that figure being there when he first walked down to take a piss in the river. But, it's dark as hell in here. I'm just getting a bit creeped out is all, Grog thought. For an instant there, didn't I hear the fucker exhale when I hit him. Let's just take it all down a notch or two. You're coming off a beer buzz, you're in a place that could, well, technically, get you into trouble with the cops, you're alone because the other Delts were too chickenshit to do it, and doing it alone would only enhance the Legend of Grog. You're going all limp over some muffled splashing sounds, and you backed into a mannequin. Get a grip for Christ sake. And about that mannequin—boy that was heavy. But these things are how old? From the looks of them—maybe 40 or 50 years. And they aren't really mannequins in the storefront sense of the word. These are more rubbery, heftier, and, probably, anchored. I bet I tore up his anchoring when I shoved him.

Something by his foot caught his eye. Grog shone the light down. A prop of some kind. A dagger. Cool. He could use something like this back at the frat house—just for shits and grins. Grog stooped to pick the dagger up by the rubber blade…and…dropped it. Son-of-a-bitch! That fucker's real, and sharp as a tack. A hair-strand line of blood appeared across Grog's fingers. Dammit. Now he'd need a tetanus shot. Real blades? What the hell kind of operation is this?

Grog had gotten so used to the splashing sounds that he suddenly noticed their absence. Now there was no sound whatsoever. Grog stood motionless. He got an irrational feeling that he was being watched. Shouldn't

101

he be hearing the sounds of the cats devouring their prey? He looked at the rivers edge, and sturdied himself. Any rodent, cat, or dog jumps out of the murkiness, and I'll drop kick its little ass across the next three displays. Grog squeezed his fist to stop the bleeding, and waited in the still darkness.

He didn't have to wait long. He recognized this noise. A boat was out there, approaching fast. Grog ran up the bank to where he'd been sitting. He peeked around the corner, to stare back at the boat path. The boat was full of mysterious shapes. Grog squinted against the darkness, afraid to use his flashlight as not to give himself away.

As they closed in, Grog could make out the front figure in the low yellow haze. The man in front seemed to be surrounded in a dense mist, fog, or…smoke. From what Grog could make out, he wore a broad-brimmed black hat and sported a long, thick…black…beard. Good god, he's looking left to right, mist swirling about his forehead, as though searching for something or…someone. A much smaller person sitting next to the apparent leader was suddenly pulling at the leader's arm. Grog's eyes moved quickly to this smaller figure. Grog couldn't say what exactly caught his heart in his throat—whether it was the fact that the goat-boy's eyes were glowing in the dark, or that the goat-boy was pointing straight toward him.

Fuck this. A billion years of genetic DNA makeup kicked into overdrive, and Grog's flight instinct took over. Grog bolted past the line of harlots he'd groped when he'd first jumped ashore, and didn't hesitate to leap back into the water, which came coldly up to his groin. Dark and greasy, it slowed him down, but upon rounding a quick curve, he was able to step up onto the platform of the next exhibit. He could barely make out the scene as he flew past, careful to slip around any dark shapes that blocked his path. He was in the water, then quickly out again onto the next display. He barely made out the scene as he turned on the afterburners. It appeared to be that of a Buccaneer prisoner trying to reach out to get the keys from a guard dog as the jailer slept next to barrels of rum.

Grog leaped out into the middle of the river, and kitty-cornered through the oily water to jump up onto the next scene. The yellow haze from the water lanterns revealed that it was the Treasure Island scenario, and he hurdled over trunks of booty—gold, silver, jewels, and pieces-of-eight. Grog dodged figures of gleeful privateers, ecstatic at their plundered riches. Then nine sluggish steps through more of the oily water brought him around the curve and onto the battle scene. This was the longest display as a mock pirate vessel on Grog's side faced-off against a British Navy ship, that lay across the river. During boat rides, captains aboard both vessels would order the railguns to be fired, puffs of smoke would shoot out of the small cannons, and fabricated water explosions would splash near the row boats.

As it was a thirty-yard dash, Grog accelerated past this display and leapt far out into the water. He was beginning to feel the fire in his lungs when he realized that he was in the tunnel. Shit. Pitch black in here. No water lanterns. If he remembered correctly, this tunnel circles around, and burns up a minute in complete darkness. It was the portion of the ride where dates got fondled.

Grog slammed into the side of the tunnel with his right shoulder. Son of a bitch. That hurt. He put his right arm out against the cold slime of the tunnel wall. Use it as a reference point. He began moving again, only this time at a turtle's pace. It was slow going wading through the shit slime, and his lungs were burning in agony.

And, as if to make matters even worse, those goddamned swimming sounds had started again. Much louder this time. Behind him, but not as far as he'd like. No way rats could make that Niagara of noise—unless there were hundreds of them. Thousands. He was at almost a walk now. Must keep moving. But he couldn't. The water was more and more difficult to plod through. His balls were freezing. Tears came to his eyes. He sucked in air, and listened as the sounds gained on him. He looked ahead and could make out a yellow lantern. Thank God. He wasn't far. Don't let up, he ordered himself, do not let up. After this tunnel ended, there was the finale. The ghost ship would lurk over the boat riders, plunging down from above, then they turn a quick corner and abruptly they'd be back at the boat launch, waiting to unload. Grog got a second wind and pushed onward. Once he made the entrance, he'd be out of here, even if he had to kick his way through the door or smash a window. He cut to his left. I'll jump up on the sand beach under the ghost ship, then I'm gone.

Something caught Grog's foot. He went down hard. The slime got in his mouth, soaked his hair. He closed his eyes, and punched toward his ankle. The pain of hard steel shot into his fist. Dammit. He'd tripped over the boat rail track. Grog burst up, coughing out water, he limped on one foot to the display. With a final ounce of strength he propelled himself up onto the long sandbar before the ship. Grog crawled several feet, then collapsed. Just let me catch my breath, he thought, gotta catch my breath. After about a minute of hyperventilation and pulling himself forward, it occurred to him that the water noise had ceased. He rolled over and stared back from whence he'd come. The river was perfectly calm, quiet—even peaceful.

As his breathing came in shorter pants, Grog began to smell a rat. Only this particular river rat had a name—Chip Davitt. He helped me plan this out, but what if he took our prank one step further? What if Chip decided to make the real prank be on Grog? That computed, all right. Face it, it made a hell of a lot more sense than the spookies and ghosts and swimming rats that

103

his imagination had conjured up in the darkness. Let's say that Chip tossed some of his daddy's green at the park owners in order to let him pull one on the Grogmeister. Hell, Chip's old man probably owns partial interest in this shit-hole amusement park. It was becoming clear now. That son-of-a-bitch had better have dry clothes, pizza and a keg of beer waiting for me in the entryway.

Grog was certain that they had cameras set up, and the Phi Delts were watching, no, they were giggling like crazy, in a control booth somewhere. Those pricks. Okay, here's how I'll play it out. It's too dark in here for the video cameras to have picked up my abject terror—especially since any monitoring cameras would only be periodically spaced. He'll tell them that he hadn't spotted goat-boy, or Blackbeard, who was, after all, Chip's favorite, and just assumed it was security coming for his sorry ass. And, by the way Chip, where did you come up with that goat-boy—he looks like something the cat screwed? After Grog'd dried off, had a couple of shots to get warm—he'd put his arm around Chip's shoulder, tell him it was a great prank, but, and this part he'd ask loud enough for the others to hear, don't you think that sticking to our original plan would have been better? He'd lost the flashlight, but Grog's last 16 ounce can of malt liquor, stuffed down the inside pocket of his school jacket, had survived the flight. Grog pulled it out, smiled broadly for any unseen cameras, and popped the top. Foam and beer suds sprayed about him.

"Chippy, Chippy, Chiparoo," Grog toasted the beer at several angles so any camera could catch him, then took a long swig. A lone, dark shape stood before the ghost ship, perhaps twenty-five feet away. Probably one of those goof-ball, animated buccaneers that waves "Goodbye" with his sword as the boats round the final curve. I bet I could hit that figure with this beer can. Grog'd like them to catch that on film, signify his coolness, and help salvage the night. There was about eight ounces of beer left, so the can could still fly. Try and peg him in the head. Grog stood up, had a final sip, took a pitcher's stance, and let fly.

Right upon Grog's release, the eyes on the lone figure began to glow. He was facing Grog, and with a casual, almost absent-minded, flip of his wrist, the cutlass came up in front of him. The malt liquor can sliced near perfectly in the middle, each half-can spraying off to a different side of the figure. From the glow off the eyes, and the yellow haze kicking up from the water lanterns, Grog recognized both the unforgiving smile and the calico pattern on the britches. In less than a heartbeat, Grog knew with certainty that this was no Chip Davitt prank.

If Grog's fear had allowed him to move, he may have seen the others approaching from behind, from the sides, and slithering out from the black

104

water. And if Grog's fear had allowed him any final thoughts, one may have been that graduation and college pranks were the least of his concerns…

Where the hell is he, Chip thought? Making us come here this early, all hung over, only to find that nothing's been rearranged. Grog hadn't returned their signals, nor did he jump back into the boat. I bet he chickened out, left, and went bar-hopping, probably hooked up with a girl or something. It'd have been nice if he'd have come back to the house, or given us a call, so we wouldn't have to have dragged our asses out here this early.

Passing the final display, Chip saw something he hadn't noticed yesterday. Although overly gory for a family-oriented amusement park, with chunks of flesh clinging to the forearms and spine, and one eye remaining in the red-tinged skull, Chip, an Art minor himself, had to appreciate the talent that had gone into creating the skeleton he watched swaying behind the wheel of the pirate ship named *Revenge*. The skeleton, hovering at the helm of the ghost ship, radiated an emotion, an eerie, forlorn aura, as if to say that steering this pirate ship was going to make for a very lonely eternity, indeed. Although the tattered rags that clung loosely to his shoulder blades and rib-cage didn't quite fit the pirate motif, they looked oddly familiar.

Suddenly it occurred to Chip. Those are our school colors.

About the Author

Jeffrey B. Burton lives in St. Paul, Minnesota with his wife, Cindy; daughter, Maddie Rose; and an over-domesticated Australian shepherd named Amber. Jeff fell in love with the short story when he read Ray Bradbury's  *The Illustrated Man* more years back than he cares to remember. Jeff has been writing for the past dozen years or so and has been fortunate to have had his lies published in *Outer Darkness, Quantum Muse, Dogwood Tales Magazine, The Cozy Detective, Potpourri, Satire, Detective Mystery Stories, Crimson,* and *Millennium Science Fiction & Fantasy Magazine.* Jeff would like to acknowledge his wife, Cindy; and father, Bruce, for letting him exploit their immeasurable editing skills.

For more information regarding Jeffrey B. Burton, visit his Web site at: www.SomeHack.com.

www.ingramcontent.com/pod-product-compliance
Lightning Source LLC
Chambersburg PA
CBHW060752180626
46818CB00002B/550